"If you are a gentleman," she asked, "why are you pinning me to the ground?"

"If you are a lady, why did you jump out of a tree?"

"It is not a short tale," she replied. "And you are heavy, sir."

"Your pardon, my lady."

No gentleman, she reasoned, would ride the streets at night wearing a mask and with a rapier at his side, yet a thief would not have begged her pardon and helped her rise.

"So your evening's work will not be a total waste," she said, plucking her pearl earrings from her ears and holding them out to him.

"Keep your ear bobs, my lady," he replied taking a step toward her. "I'll take this instead."

Gripping her small shoulders between her hands, he kissed her, very quickly but very thoroughly. And then he vaulted over the wall and into the darkness.

CAPTAIN RAKEHELL

Jane Lynson

FAWCETT CREST • NEW YORK

A Fawcett Crest Book
Published by Ballantine Books
Copyright © 1989 by Lynne Smith

Library of Congress Catalog Card Number: 89-91400

ISBN 0-449-21724-8

Manufactured in the United States of America

First Edition: January 1990

Chapter One

If he hadn't tripped over a muddy, grass-stained slipper beneath the thick-limbed beech tree in the farthermost corner of the garden behind the Dowager Duchess of Braxton's elegant Bond Street mansion, Andrew Gilbertson, the Viscount Welsey, never would have found his twin. In the smoky glimmer of the lantern he'd filched from the stables when he'd looked there for his sister, he saw that the slipper and its mate—turned on one side a half pace to his right—were indeed the same rosy shade of pink as Amanda's gown.

"Gave yourself away leaving your shoes down here," Andrew said, frowning as he raised the lantern.

The feeble light it cast only just reached the second crotch of the old tree, where his twin sister, Lady Amanda Gilbertson, sat on a broad limb with her back against the main trunk. Her skirts were gathered up around her knees, exposing her slim calves and delicate ankles. The hem of her gown, torn and muddy, shimmered in the flickering glow of the lantern.

1

"I tucked my slippers in my bodice," Amanda replied, leaning on her right arm to look down at her brother, "but they fell out on the way up."

"Wouldn't have if you *had* a bodice."

Laughing good-naturedly, Amanda leaned farther out over the limb to grin at Andrew. Her Grecian curls, so painstakingly styled by her dresser, had fallen against her shoulder in wispy loops that gleamed a deep, burnished red in the lantern light.

"Insult me, Andy, and you insult yourself."

Which was true enough. Though Andrew was much taller, a hair's breadth over six feet, with an admirably fine chest (which Amanda had always thought should have been hers), the rest of their features—classically flawless nose, lofty cheekbones, and slightly dimpled chin—and their rich mahogany brown hair and sapphire blue eyes, were exactly alike.

Had they been the same sex the Gilbertson twins would have been identical. As it was, they were and had been throughout their nearly one and twenty years, virtually inseparable. Until this moment, Andrew had always thought his mother's dire warnings about Amanda being allowed to share his tutors and his riding and shooting lessons silly and unfounded. But the sight of her astraddle the limb, her hair in disarray, and her gown—the cost of which had prompted Lord Hampton to ring for a whiskey—in tatters, he wished he and his father had listened.

"Couldn't you have found a place to hide from Captain Earnshaw that wouldn't have ruined your gown and your hair?"

"I am not hiding from that loathsome man," Amanda replied mildly, as she settled herself against the trunk again. "I am simply waiting for the stars to fall."

Andrew glanced up at the night sky. Astronomy had never been his best subject, yet he'd gleaned enough of the science to know there was very little chance Polaris would tumble out of its place in Ursa Minor.

"I think you're going to have a long wait, Mandy. They look pretty firmly fixed to me."

"You goose!" She laughed. "I don't mean *all* the stars, just some of them. Or perhaps little pieces of them. Although Charles isn't at all sure—"

"Charles!" Andrew cried, taken aback. "Is this the kind of thing he writes to you about?"

"Well, of course it is," Amanda returned, glancing down at him curiously.

"The Duke of Braxton writes to you about falling stars—not falling in love?"

"Andy!" Amanda breathed indignantly. "Charles is a *gentleman!* It would be highly *indelicate* for him to confide his affairs to me!"

"Oh, bloody hell!" Andrew sagged against the beech on one shoulder, the lantern sputtering as it clanked against the trunk. "If I'd had any idea what you were up to, Mandy, I would never have agreed to be your go-between!"

"Go-between?" she echoed. "How could you even consider that passing on the letters Charles sends to me in your name *only* because Mama and Papa would decree it unseemly for a man of his age and rank to correspond with me as playing the go-between?"

Her brother didn't answer, just swept one hand over his eyes and shook his head. His reaction spoke volumes to Amanda, who began to laugh, so richly and so wildly that she nearly fell out of the tree.

"Oh, Andy, you nodcock!" Still laughing, she caught an overhead branch and used it to right herself on her perch. "Charles is interested in my *mind*, not my *hand*!"

If Charles Earnshaw, the Duke of Braxton and Captain Lord Lesley Earnshaw's older brother, would but once raise his head from the musty books in his library, Andrew thought ruefully, he would see that Amanda, whose bare, dangling legs gleamed like alabaster in the lantern glow, had more than a mind to interest him.

"From the way you two had your heads together at the dowager duchess's last house party," he said testily, as he set the lantern down on the spongy ground, "I thought you had formed an attachment!"

"We have, but not of *that* sort," Amanda retorted loftily. "Charles and I share common interests in science and history and languages and—"

"Then what in blazes are you doing in that tree?"

"Don't ring a peal over *me*, Andrew Gilbertson! And I've already told you what I'm doing up here!"

"Why couldn't you step out on the terrace to watch the stars fall?"

"Because then, you dunce head, Captain Earnshaw would be able to find me!"

"Aha!" Andrew flung an accusatory index finger at his sister. "You admit you're hiding!"

"Of course I am!" Amanda shot back, her eyes flashing angrily. "You know I *loathe* Lesley Earnshaw! He's a toadeater and a wretch! One minute so fawningly nice to me I could gag, and the next sneaking behind me to pull my hair or put a bug down my back!"

"For heaven's sake," Andrew spat exasperatedly, "that was ten years ago! We were children!"

"What about the night he tied my dress sash to my chair, and after dinner I couldn't stand up? Or the day he slipped a cocklebur under your pony's saddle and he threw you?"

"I admit Lesley was a bit of a prankster—"

"A prankster!" Amanda cried. "He's a bully! Why, when we were only eleven and he was sixteen, he blacked your eye! Or have you forgotten that?"

"I forget what sent Lesley and me at each other, but I *do* remember that I was quite holding my own until *you* jumped into the fracas to save me! And none of this, Mandy, has any bearing whatsoever on you being up a tree!"

"Which is precisely where I am, metaphorically as well as physically," she retorted. "Because I've been out for three Seasons and Papa hasn't been deluged with offers for me, he and Mama think I'm hopelessly on the shelf! Don't be deceived, Andy, that's why they're determined to marry me off to Lesley Earnshaw, because the shame of a spinster in the family is too much for them! In their opinion, it's far better I be married to such a vile Master Jacaanapes than never married at all!"

"Mandy," Andrew said patiently. "You haven't seen Lesley since he blacked my eye, since before he went up to Oxford and then into the Dragoons. He's a war hero! He fought quite bravely in the Peninsula and at Waterloo—"

"He's also fought two duels," Amanda interrupted, "and has kept a string of high steppers!"

"Good God!" Andrew exploded. "Who teaches you words like that?"

"*You* do, cloth head!"

Indeed he did, Andrew recollected, only vaguely able to recall the last time he'd come in cup shot

5

from his club, and Amanda had taken advantage of his well-corned state to wheedle the latest cant phrases out of him.

"Well, you shouldn't repeat them," he blustered. "And if you value my life, you won't let on to Captain Earnshaw that you know about his—er—connections among the muslin company."

"I won't betray you, Andy. Why, without you, I should be totally ignorant of the ways of men and women."

"And promise me you won't tell Mama you know anything about *that*, either."

"Anything about what?"

"The—ah"—he paused to clear his throat—"ways of men and women."

"Of course I won't! I shouldn't want to confuse her."

"But *especially* promise you won't breathe a word to Captain Earnshaw."

"Don't worry, Andy. I can't possibly breathe a word of anything to a man I have no intention of *ever* speaking to!"

"Mandy," Andrew spoke her name sharply, his patience growing thin. "You can't stay up in that tree forever."

"No, I can't," she agreed. "But there are lots of other trees in London, *hundreds* at Hampton Hall, and absolute hundreds of *thousands* all over England. If necessary I'll climb every last one of them to evade Lesley Earnshaw!"

And she would, too. Andrew knew his sister, and the resolute set of her jaw, as well as he knew himself.

"You're being childish, Mandy," he said forcefully. "Stop it this instant and come down from there."

"When the ball is over and everyone's gone home I'll come down, but not a second before."

"Papa is turning the duchess's house topsy-turvy looking for you, and Mama is beside herself. You must come down!"

"I won't!" Amanda declared fiercely.

"Lesley hasn't even arrived yet, and at this late hour he isn't likely to! Now come down!"

"No!"

"Very well. Then you leave me no choice but to bring you down."

It took him two tries, but Andrew finally leaped high enough to catch the lowest limb of the ancient beech. How Amanda, even though she was two parts monkey when it came to climbing trees, had managed it, he couldn't fathom. Grunting, he swung his right leg over the limb, levered himself into a sitting position, and looked up to see that his sister had scrambled from the second to the third crotch. There was only one more above her; beyond that, the branches were considerably thinner and much farther between.

"Don't even think it," Andrew warned breathlessly.

"I'll climb to the very top and jump," she threatened, "before I'll let you drag me in there to be married against my will!"

"There's no parson on the guest list, Mandy." He paused to catch his wind and consider a new tactic. "You've been quite the envy of the evening, you know, even in your absence. All the marriageable young ladies are saying how positively green they are that you've captured Captain Earnshaw sight unseen."

"What?" Amanda shrieked. "Mama swore she'd keep mum!"

"Er, well, perhaps I misunderstood."

"And perhaps you've sided with Mama and Papa against me!" Amanda climbed two branches higher and glared down at him reproachfully. "How *could* you, Andy!"

"Don't be totty-headed! Of course I haven't sided against you! But hiding in trees will do you no good. What if Papa comes looking in the garden? Or Mama, or—"

"Shhh!" Amanda hissed, pressing a finger to her lips.

Andrew heard it then, a faint rustling of stealthy footsteps in the shrubbery outside the low wall that enclosed the garden. It was faint, yet growing closer to the beech tree, whose limbs overhung the bushes and the gate in the wall. There would be no need for his father, he realized, or any of the other guests to move so furtively.

From the proximity of the footsteps, Andrew gauged he hadn't time enough to get Amanda down and safely into the house. Dropping noiselessly to the ground, he extinguished the lantern, swung himself up into the beech again, and climbed to a stout limb just one below Amanda. She laid her right hand, her fingers trembling, on his shoulder.

There was a thump and a muffled crash in the bushes just outside the gate. Amanda started, her fingers digging painfully into Andrew's collarbone.

" 'Arry, you idget!" spat a hoarse, low voice. "Keep yer damn big dew beaters out from under mine, will ya?"

"Sorry, Jack, sorry!" Harry answered tremulously. "Didn' see you'd stopped, s'all. Bloody damn dark t'night!"

He pronounced it 'noight,' and the fact that he and Jack were skulking in the shrubbery told Andrew they were up to no good. The gate rattled, and Amanda's fingers dug deeper into his shoulder. Wincing, he loosened her grip.

" 'Ere's the gate, then. We'll wait 'ere for 'im like 'e said."

"We could climb over, Jack. This 'ere wall ain't n'more 'an four feet."

There was a thump and a yowl in the bushes.

"We ain't s'posed t'be seen, ya idget! We's t'wait 'ere on this side 'o the wall 'til 'e whistles us over t'take the loot from 'im."

"Sorry, Jack. I forgot s'all."

"All right, then," Jack grumbled. "Now dub yer mummer."

Twigs snapped and leaves crackled as Harry and Jack settled down in the bushes to wait.

"Can't we climb down and sneak past them?" Amanda asked, her voice so low Andrew could barely hear her.

"Not with you in a satin gown," he whispered. "Your skirts would make more racket than the shrubbery."

"We just can't sit here," she hissed in his ear. "They mean to rob the house! And perhaps *all* the guests! Mama and Papa could be in danger!"

"Be *still*, Mandy. These are desperate men. Our best course is to sit here and keep quiet until they've gone away."

"But, Andy—"

Twisting around, Andrew clapped his hand over Amanda's mouth.

"Dub yer mummer," he muttered, "or you'll give us away."

Chapter Two

Despite his advanced state of inebriation, Captain Lord Lesley Earnshaw executed two masterful thrusts with his rapier before turning somewhat wobbily to face his younger brothers. Although he could only remember one Teddy in the family, the fact that there were two blurred and worried-looking faces gazing back at him in the dim lantern light seemed just the tiniest bit strange.

"Have you always been twins?" he asked puzzledly.

"No, Lesley, I'm not twins." Theodore Earnshaw, the youngest of the Dowager Duchess of Braxton's three sons, grasped and shook his brother's shoulders. "Amanda Gilbertson is a twin. Remember Amanda? Your soon-to-be betrothed?"

"Amanda ... my betrothed ..." The captain's handsome face furrowed thoughtfully as he raised his right hand, which still held the rapier, to scratch his tousled dark hair.

The blade whizzed past Teddy's head, just missing his left ear. He ducked, then turned to his friend, Lyndon Smithers, who stood in the shadows holding a small water keg and wooden tankard borrowed from the coachman who'd driven them down to London to attend Captain Earnshaw's welcome home ball.

"Time for drastic measures," Teddy announced. "Fill the cup and stand back."

"You'd best do the same," Lyndon advised, as he poured the tankard full and passed it.

"I intend to," Teddy replied, retreating a safe distance before letting the water fly.

Because the captain stood on the very edge of the aura cast by the lantern, puzzling over why his mother had given the twins the same name, he didn't see the toss coming. It caught him full in the face, startling and unbalancing him. His knee-high Hessians shot out from under him on the dew-soaked grass, and he sat down heavily with a yowl of pain. Clutching his left buttock, he rolled onto his stomach, gasping, gritting his teeth, and becoming suddenly sober.

As he laid there, spluttering and cursing not only his brother but the cross-eyed Froggy who'd aimed his musket to unman him, but instead had only unhorsed him (praise God), Teddy cupped one hand around his mouth and called softly into the darkness: "Hallo, Forbes! Having any luck with Hawksley?"

A young man of about Teddy's eighteen years leaned his charge against a stout-boled elm and stepped into the misty glow of the half-dozen lanterns illuminating the center of this remote glade in Regent's Park. As he did so, Sir Alex Hawksley slid slowly to the ground and slumped on his left side. Forbes called back: "Not a whit's worth!"

"Hang on! I'll send Smithers with the water! Lyndon?"

"On my way," he replied, the keg sloshing in his arms as he jogged away.

Gingerly easing himself into a right-sided sitting position, Earnshaw reached inside his unbuttoned waistcoat for a handkerchief, but instead pulled out a black silk mask. The light from the lantern winking through the eye holes brought the wine-clouded earlier portion of the evening back to him: drinking his dinner at his club on his way to Bond Street and the ball his mother had contrived to introduce him to Lady Amanda Gilbertson; falling in with Sir Alex and repairing to Madame Sophia's masquerade; discovering Teddy there in the arms of one of Madame's Cyprians, unmasking him and ringing a peal over him, Hawksley saying . . . something . . . insulting about Charles. . . .

"Teddy?"

"Yes, Lesley?"

"Did Hawksley actually refer to our brother as His Dottiness?"

"He did. But as I tried to tell you at Madame Sophia's, Charles knows everyone calls him the Dotty Duke, and actually thinks it's quite amusing."

"Does he?" Earnshaw laid his elbows on his knees and glowered at his younger brother. "I wonder if he'd think finding you at Madame's amusing?"

"As I also tried to tell you," Teddy replied defensively, "I *did* go to Charles and ask him to—er—arrange something for me, but it flustered him so—"

"That you took the matter into your own hands," Earnshaw finished, cocking one eyebrow. "So to speak."

"Yes, so to speak." Teddy sighed wistfully, recalling the lush redhead whose arms Lesley had wrenched him out of. "I don't see why you couldn't have allowed me another half—no, make that three-quarters of an hour."

"Because, Teddy," Earnshaw replied tiredly, as he raked his wet hair off his forehead, "a boy your age has no idea of the trouble he can get into in a place like Madame's."

"Of course I do!" Teddy cried indignantly. "It's why I was there! But now, thanks to you, I'm here instead!"

"Just precisely where *is* here, by the way?" Earnshaw asked, glancing around him at the trees enclosing the glade and the wisps of ground fog drifting between them.

"Regent's Park. Madame suggested it. She also suggested rapiers—"

"To avoid bringing the whole of Bow Street down on us, yes, I remember now. Something about the Runners keeping a watchful eye on her establishment for gentlemen who leave there with scores to settle."

"It was also Madame's suggestion that we adjourn here straightaway, because the Runners periodically keep dawn watches at the usual fields."

"A wise woman, Madame," sighed Earnshaw. "Well, I suppose we should get on with it then."

"Are you all right, now?" Teddy asked, as he helped his brother to his feet.

"Other than being thoroughly soaked, I seem to be."

"Sorry, Lesley, but when mention of Amanda Gilbertson couldn't rouse you from your stupor, I hadn't any choice."

"Since I am now roused," the Captain growled,

13

"I'll thank you not to mention the chit's name until I contrive a way to make her cry off."

"I've thought of a way." Teddy grinned and folded his arms. "Simply carve up Hawksley and bruit it about that it was your swordsmanship that left him looking like a Christmas goose."

"Think of another one," Earnshaw suggested with a pointed glance. "I've no wish to see the inside of Newgate, thank you, and I've been to France."

A howl of outrage drew their attention to the opposite side of the glade, and to Lyndon and Forbes fleeing Sir Alex, who lurched to his feet spitting water and epithets.

"I say, Hawksley!" Earnshaw called quietly. "You might recall the point of this is secrecy, so if you wouldn't mind—stifle it!"

"Right you are," replied Sir Alex, as he shook the water off himself. "A moment and I'll be with you."

"At your leisure."

"Perhaps," Teddy suggested brightly, "your not showing up at mother's ball tonight will put Amanda off."

"Doubtful." Carefully, Captain Earnshaw wiped the blade of his rapier on his buff-colored pantaloons. "If she's been out—how many Seasons did you say?"

"Three."

"Three Seasons, then, with no offers, she's undoubtedly desperate." He stepped closer to the lantern to examine the rapier, the tallowy light streaking his still-wet raven hair with blue highlights. "Tell the truth, Teddy. How ugly did she grow up to be?"

"Not very," he lied, hiding the grin on his face

behind a hastily cupped hand. "And she's had offers, Lesley. One that I know of—perhaps even two."

"Why the devil did Lord Hampton refuse them?" A lock of hair fell over the captain's drawn-together eyebrows as he ran the flat of his thumb lightly up the edge of the blade.

"According to Andrew he didn't—it was Amanda."

"For heaven's sake why?" Earnshaw asked mildly, as he took several practice cuts.

"I'm not at liberty to say."

"Is that so?"

The rapier flashed in the backwash of the lantern and came to rest with its tip just pricking Teddy's neckcloth. Despite the grin on his face, the boy swallowed hard.

"Since you ask so politely, then," he said, lying baldly as he eased the unresisting blade away from his throat. "According to Andrew, Amanda is holding fast to the attachment she formed for you in childhood."

"Teddy." Earnshaw said threateningly, bringing the tip of the rapier again to his throat.

"I swear it's the truth, Lesley. On our father's grave I swear it."

He made the vow knowing that their father, the Master of every Jacaanapes ever born, would forgive him; and that the lie was the very least Lesley deserved for depriving him of his luscious redhead.

"Oh, dear God," Earnshaw sighed, the rapier going limp in his hand.

"I'd sooner you killed me now," Teddy said, stepping in front of the wilted blade, "as let on to Amanda that I've told you. I gave Andrew my word I wouldn't, you know."

"I won't betray you, Teddy," Earnshaw said soberly, frowning as he resheathed his blade. "Damn and blast! I could have sworn she loathed me."

"Oh, *no!*" Teddy assured him quickly. "You should have seen her, Lesley, when we read in the Dispatches that the Second had captured an Eagle. Why, her breast nearly burst with pride! Amanda is convinced you secured the standard single-handedly."

Making a noise in his throat, the captain forked his hands through his hair and turned away.

"Frankly, Lesley," Teddy went on blithely, "I can't think of a single thing that would turn Amanda's affections. She's quite convinced that you are the handsomest, bravest cove that ever—"

"What'd you say?" Earnshaw interrupted, spinning sharply on one heel.

"I said I can't think of a single—"

"No, no—tell me again what Amanda thinks."

"I said she thinks you're the handsomest, bravest—"

"That's it!" The captain grinned and clasped his brother's shoulders. "Bless you, Teddy! You've saved me from a parson's mousetrap!"

"I have?" He asked blankly. "How'd I do that?"

"Very well, Earnshaw!" Hawksley called gruffly. "Ready when you are!"

"Just coming!" The captain gave Teddy an affectionate jostle. "Later, lad."

Perplexed, Teddy hurried to keep pace with Lesley as he strode, whistling under his breath, toward the lanterns lighting the middle of the glade. Lyndon had withdrawn to one of the sidelines, where he sat on the water keg to keep watch. Forbes, who'd come down in the coach with Teddy and Smithers, followed from the far side of the glade behind his cousin Hawksley.

"Here we are then, Alex." Earnshaw stopped a few paces short of his opponent. "I'll give you one last chance to recant."

"Not much point since we're already out here," Hawksley replied, as he drew his rapier. "But I'll say this much—you're going to be a busy fellow, Lesley, if you call out everyone who dubs Charles His Dottiness."

"I think not." The captain grinned, taking his blade in hand and squaring off on Hawksley. "Once word gets round of how easily I sliced you up for beefsteak, I'm sure the term will fall out of fashion."

"Oh ho!" Sir Alex laughed, taking his stance. "Brave words!"

"Am I supposed to be doing something?" Teddy asked, the gleam in his brother's eyes making him nervous.

"Just keep out of the way," Earnshaw replied, his gaze fixed intently on Hawksley, as the slightly taller but much heavier man began to circle him.

"Don't have to tell me twice," Forbes said, catching Teddy's elbow and drawing him clear of the lanterns.

"I'll give you first strike, Alex," the captain offered, wincing a bit as he shifted his weight onto the balls of his feet and felt the muscles in his left leg tighten.

"First and last," replied Hawksley, feinting, and then following with a deft inside thrust.

Just as deftly, Earnshaw deflected it and countered with a lightning quick stroke that sliced Sir Alex's left sleeve near the shoulder. Hawksley glanced down at the blood staining his linen and tightened his grip on his rapier.

"Thought you'd be rusty, Lesley."

"Think again, Alex."

More cautiously this time, Hawksley circled, looking for a weakness. Earnshaw's pulse was thudding with excitement so loudly inside his head that he didn't hear his brother's shout, wasn't aware that he'd even spoken until Sir Alex lowered his blade and glanced toward the sideline. The captain turned then, as Teddy and Forbes and Smithers came pelting toward them.

"Runners!" Teddy cried. "Three of them, working their way this direction!"

"Damn!" Earnshaw spat, more disappointed than alarmed, as he sheathed his rapier. "We'll have to finish this another time, Alex."

"So we will, Lesley." Hawksley, too, put away his rapier, then said to Forbes, "Stay with your chums, lad, and get yourselves back to your coach quick as you can."

"Come *on!*" Teddy cried urgently, tugging at his brother's arm. "They're *coming!*"

Though he wasn't overly concerned—Bow Street rarely made trouble over duels between gentlemen—Earnshaw allowed Teddy to pull him into a limping run toward the stand of elms where he and Hawksley had left their horses. As they entered the trees, a gruff voice called from the far side of the dense copse: "You there! *Hold!*"

"The bloody hell I will!" Earnshaw shouted back.

In answer, there came the snap and rustle of heavy feet moving rapidly toward them through the wood.

"Damn buggers have us surrounded!" Hawksley cried, his voice ringing with outrage, as he untied and mounted his bay gelding.

"Go, Lesley!" Teddy urged, pushing his brother toward his prancing, excited black.

"And leave you to face a pack of Runners?" Stumbling against his horse, Earnshaw caught hold of the saddle but refused to mount. "Not likely!"

"What can they do to me if *you* aren't here?" Teddy unlashed the reins securing his brother's stallion to a stout sapling and shoved them into his hands. "And think what mother will do if she finds out about this!"

"He's right," Hawksley agreed. "Without our presence to incriminate them, the lads will be safe enough."

He dug his heels into the bay's flanks, then, and the gelding leaped away. Earnshaw's stallion tried to bolt with him, and while the captain fumbled to gather his reins and steady the ready to run thoroughbred, Teddy grabbed his left boot heel and tossed him into the saddle. Taken off guard, Earnshaw had no choice but to catch the stirrups and snatch the bit out of Lucifer's teeth to keep him from rearing.

"Meet me at mother's house," Teddy told him, "in the stables. I'll bring you a change of clothes."

"Too late," Earnshaw replied, looking over the stallion's ears at the three figures striding into the lantern-lit glade. "Bright as daylight out there, they'll see me for sure."

"My mask from Madame Sophia's!" Teddy cried, jumping up and down and trying to pluck it out of Lesley's waistcoat. "Put it on! Quickly!"

In an effort to calm his brother and Lucifer, who were both just this side of apoplexy, Earnshaw took the leathers in his teeth, drew out the mask and tied it around his head. As he did so, Teddy backed away from the stallion, drew back his arm and slapped him as hard as he could on the rump.

Snorting and laying back his ears, Lucifer sprang

half-up on his hind legs, then shot out of the trees at a full gallop. The Runners crossing the glade gave way as the stallion thundered toward them flinging clods of turf from under his hooves.

As he turned to duck into the trees, Teddy cast a last glance at Lucifer galloping his brother to safety. At the sight of Lesley rising from his saddle to stand in his stirrups, he began to laugh. And then he began to run.

Chapter Three

Warm as the early evening had been, by midnight it was decidedly chilly in the upper reaches of the beech tree. Andrew gallantly gave Amanda his coat, but the thin, satin-lined evening jacket was little protection against the damp in the thick fog gathering at the foot of the old tree.

"I've been thinking," Amanda whispered, her teeth chattering in her brother's ear. "I could stay here and keep watch on Jack and Harry while you go for help."

"No, Mandy," Andrew whispered sternly. "I will not leave you unprotected."

"I'll be perfectly safe up here—"

"No," Andrew repeated. "It'll be soon now, I think. If I were the thief, I'd strike while the guests were dining."

Almost as he spoke the words, the music drifting from the house stopped, signaling that supper had been announced. A rustle in the shrubbery and a few guttural words exchanged by Harry and Jack confirmed the veracity of Andrew's statement.

"We should climb lower," Amanda whispered, "so we can see their faces."

"We'll do no such thing."

"But how will we be able to identify them?"

"Identifying them is not our responsibility."

"Then whose is it, I should like to know?"

" 'Ere now, what's that?" Jack growled, the bushes snapping loudly. "You 'ear somethin', 'Arry?"

Andrew froze, but Amanda didn't. Seizing the opportunity, she caught an overhead branch and used it to swing herself around the trunk to the opposite side of the tree. Too late, Andrew heard the telltale whisper of her satin skirts. He twisted on the limb to catch her, just as the last torn inch of the hem of her gown slipped out of his reach.

"There it is a'gin," Jack said, his tone low and wary. "You 'ear anythin', 'Arry?"

"Jus' th' wind, Jack, murmurin' in that big ol' tree."

"Th' wind ain't blowin', ya idget."

"It ain't?"

A thump and howl came from the bushes, as Andrew inched around the trunk and saw Amanda, standing sure-footed on a thick limb several feet below him. As he watched her, she leaned cautiously forward and caught the trailing end of her gown. Drawing the skirt up between her legs, she tucked it into her waist sash.

Andrew groaned silently. He'd seen his sister secure her skirts thus hundreds of times, usually before flinging herself astraddle onto her pony, climbing into the loft of the barn at Hampton Hall, or wading into the creek. Heaven only knew what she was preparing for now, but whatever it was, it was his duty—as it always had been—to save her from herself. Sighing, he climbed after her.

The scrape of his foot on a branch above her alerted Amanda to his approach. Flinging a glare at him, she swung herself one limb lower. Andrew held up a hand to reassure her, then wedged himself into the crotch she'd just vacated.

"No lower," he hissed, and she nodded.

Gauging they were still a good fifteen feet or so from the steaming ground—and hoping it would be a safe enough distance—Andrew turned his attention to the Duchess of Braxton's mansion. He heard Jack and Harry's accomplice before he saw him, and realized as the figure stepped into the backwash of the lights blazing from the house, that the dull clanking he'd heard came from the sack thrown over the man's left shoulder. He realized, too, that the angle of his approach would bring him directly beneath the beech tree, where Amanda's slippers and the lantern still lay on the ground. Andrew caught and held his breath.

So did Amanda, but for an entirely different reason. Noble as she thought Andy was for putting her safety above apprehending these criminals, she had no intention of allowing them to escape. She, too, had realized that the thief hurrying across the garden must pass directly beneath them to reach the gate in the wall where Harry and Jack awaited him. She intended to drop out of the tree onto his head, which, of course, would give Andy no choice but to jump after her to save her from these desperate men.

Not that she thought they were—at least not Jack and Harry—but she'd chosen not to argue the point with Andy. If she'd learned nothing else in the three luckless Seasons since her come out, Amanda

23

had learned that gentlemen didn't like being made fools of by females.

Almost running now, the sack flung over his shoulder making an awful racket, the thief drew within ten feet of the beech tree. Her heart pounding and her palms nervously damp, Amanda gripped the limb upon which she crouched.

"Hallo, Smythe!" Jack called from the shrubbery. "S'that you?"

"Who else you expectin'? Prinney 'Imself?" Smythe replied, as he drew nearer to Amanda and she wiggled closer to the edge of the limb.

Just as she gathered herself to jump, Smythe tripped and fell face-first on the spongy, muddy grass. The sack spilled off his shoulder, slid down the short slope of ground to the garden wall, and came to rest there with a clunk.

What luck! He's already down, Amanda thought, all I have to do is hold him there. But as she let go of the limb to jump, Andrew caught a handful of his coat and held her fast.

"Andy!" She gasped, trying to twist herself free. "We can catch them if—"

Slipping his right arm up and under hers, Andrew clapped his hand over his sister's mouth, and wrapped his left arm half around the beech trunk. "We could also catch a knife in the ribs," he hissed in her ear.

" 'Ere, Smythe!" Jack called. "What's 'appened?"

"I tripped on somethin'," Smythe replied, feeling the ground around him as he reared back on his heels. "Git over 'ere wi'th' lamp."

There was a flare of light in the bushes, which faded suddenly—probably as Jack slipped a hood over the lantern, Andrew guessed—then the scrape

24

of heavy boots on stone. Two figures, dimly outlined in the half light, clambered over the wall. The larger one bent to retrieve the sack, flung it with a clank over his shoulder, then joined his two fellows under the tree.

"What's this?" Smythe said, as he got to his feet and stepped closer to the shrouded lantern. "Lift th' shade a bit, Jack."

Andrew groaned as a thin beam of light fell on Amanda's muddy shoe, and the gold braid trim on the sleeve of the peacock blue Braxton livery worn by Smythe. But that's all he saw, for the light was too feeble to illuminate the thieves' faces.

"A ladies' slipper!" Jack exclaimed. "What you s'pose it's doin' 'ere?"

Harry stepped closer to have a look, stumbled, and bumped into Jack.

" 'Arry, you idget!"

"Look, Jack!" Harry bent down and came up with Amanda's other shoe. " 'Ere's th' other'un!"

"Gimme that." Smythe snatched it away from him and held the slippers close to the lantern. "It's a matched pair, all right. One could be a cast off, er lost, but the two of 'em . . ."

Slowly, he raised his face to the beech tree. It was too dark to make out his features, and Andrew, who tightened his grip on Amanda as she began to tremble, prayed it was also too dark for Smythe to see them.

"Jack, lift th' shade a bit more'n shine it up this tree."

"Righto," he said, tugging at the shrouded lantern. "Demmed thing's stuck!" He grunted, the globe rattling and the beam of light wobbling as he tried to loosen the hood.

"*Now*, Mandy," Andrew whispered urgently.

25

"Crawl as far as you can out this limb, then jump and run to the house!"

Shoving her away from him, he dove out of the beech tree. His elbow caught Jack in the chin as he landed, and knocked him topsy-turvy down the slope. The lantern rolled out of his grasp, broke with a splintering crash, and set fire to the pile of dead leaves blown up against the wall. Rolling clear of the small blaze, Jack came to his feet and started slipping his way back up the slope.

"Andy!" Amanda screamed at her brother, who'd turned toward Smythe with raised fists. "Behind you!"

As Andrew whirled to meet the charge, Harry dropped the sack and rushed to help Jack. He lost his footing on the wet grass, however, and crashed to the ground taking Jack with him. They rolled back down the hill in a tangle, Jack howling as his left arm was flung into the burning leaves.

"Andy! Watch out!" Amanda shrieked, as her brother turned once more toward Smythe, and spun squarely into the thief's doubled right fist.

The blow snapped his neck and staggered him against the beech tree. Amanda heard the back of his head strike the trunk with a thud, and she shrieked again as he crumpled and slid slowly to the ground. Over Jack's pitiful mewling and the slap of Harry's hands beating at his smoldering sleeve, Amanda heard Smythe chuckle as he stepped beneath the tree and glanced up at her. Though she'd leaned as far over the limb as she dared, the low, smoking fire was too far away to show her more than the sheen of perspiration on his face.

"An' who might you be, m'lady?"

"Amanda Gilbertson!" She declared fiercely. "Daughter of the Earl of Hampton!"

"Take m'word fer it, m'lady," Smythe replied, gesturing toward Andy. "Spirited 'lil thing like you c'n do better 'an a cove what can't take a punch."

"That cove is my brother!"

"Is 'e now?" Smythe chuckled, as he bent to retrieve the sack Harry had dropped.

Furious at his innuendo, determined to avenge Andy, and certain—at least reasonably so—that Smythe wouldn't *dare* strike a lady of Quality, Amanda flung back her arms and jumped.

In that same instant, Lucifer came soaring over the garden wall with Captain Earnshaw standing in his stirrups and leaning over his neck. Jack and Harry, who'd put out the fire on Jack's sleeve and gotten partway to their feet, flung themselves down again, and thereby missed having their necks broken. As the stallion's hooves touched ground, his shoulder caught Smythe in the back, knocked the sack from his hands and spun him around—just as Amanda came plummeting earthward and swept Captain Earnshaw out of his saddle.

They fell in a heap of swirling, rose-pink satin, the horseman crying out as her little ladyship landed on his chest and began pummeling him with her fists. Mistaking the yelp of pain as a call for reinforcements, Smythe quickly hied himself over the wall and into the darkness beyond. Jack and Harry followed, the sack of loot half spilled and forgotten on the ground behind them.

"Ouch! Damn you! Stop it!"

Grasping her wrists, Earnshaw arched his back and easily reversed their positions. For a moment, until he shook his head, closed his eyes, and opened them again, he thought the fall had more than

27

stunned him—but the heart-shaped, fire-lit face glaring up at him belligerently was still that of a woman. A small and remarkably strong one, he thought ruefully, his jaw still stinging from her blows.

"I'm not afraid of you," she said, her voice trembling. "All thieves are cowards or they wouldn't be thieves."

"Why on earth would you think me a thief?"

"Although you speak like a gentleman," she replied, "you are wearing a mask."

She said it matter-of-factly, but the tremor in her voice had spread to her wrists. They felt quite small and delicate in his hands, her skin as soft as the silk-lined sleeves rolled up her forearms. In the dull glow of the fire, her loosened hair gleamed a deep, burnished red. Dirt smudged her face, her gown, and the too-large man's evening jacket she wore over it. It struck him then that she hadn't screamed or swooned or threatened him with either one. And despite her claim to the contrary, her wide, unblinking eyes and the rapid rise and fall of her small bosom told him she was terrified.

"Would my lady believe," he asked, "that I've just come from a masquerade?"

"No. There are no masquerades being held this evening."

"This particular one," Earnshaw chuckled, "was not a Society affair."

She blinked at that, twice, very rapidly, but otherwise held his gaze.

"If you are a gentleman," she asked, "why are you pinning me to the ground?"

"If you are a lady, why did you jump out of a tree?"

"It is not a short tale," she replied, her eyes—a

28

deep shade of blue, he thought—luminous in the half dark. "And you are heavy, sir."

"Your pardon, my lady."

Reluctantly, Earnshaw rose and helped her to her feet. The top of her head came no higher than the first button of his muddy, ruined waistcoat. He still held her hands, could still feel the warmth of her small body against his.

The fire started by Jack's lantern had smoldered down to the wet humus at the bottom of the pile. Smoke billowed up the slope, wrapping them in the sharp smell of burned leaves and damp earth. It tickled Amanda's nose, yet freeing her hands from those of the masked man to rub it never occurred to her.

No gentleman, she reasoned, would ride the streets at night in a mask with a rapier at his side, yet a thief would not have begged her pardon and helped her rise. A gentleman most definitely would *not* have held her to the ground in such a shockingly intimate fashion, still—

Just then, Andrew groaned and stirred in the leaves beneath the beech tree. Stiffening, the masked man loosed her hands and reached for his rapier.

"It's all right, he's my brother," she said, lifting her skirts and scurrying to his side.

He was still sprawled half against the bole and still unconscious, but he groaned again and coughed in the thickening smoke as Earnshaw dropped to one knee at his feet.

"What happened to him?"

"Your friend Smythe hit him and he fell against the tree," Amanda replied, chafing one of Andrew's limp hands between her own.

"I know no one named Smythe, my lady."

"Oh, of course not," she retorted, eyeing him sharply over her brother's slumped form.

If indeed he was her brother, which the captain doubted. He'd cajoled more than one young lady into a dark garden himself, but never his sister. He'd never had a sister, but that fact made her explanation no less suspicious, perhaps because he wished he'd been the one to lure her into the darkness.

"And I don't suppose," Amanda went on, "you know anyone named Jack or Harry, do you?"

"As a matter of fact, my lady, I do not."

She made a derisive noise in her throat, which turned into a cough as a particularly acrid puff of smoke from the smoldering leaves billowed around them. Tears welled in her eyes, and the man under the tree stirred again and coughed.

"We should remove your—er, brother," Earnshaw said, leaning over Andrew to pick him up. "This smoke can't be doing him any good. Or you either, my lady."

"No!" Amanda cried, just as there came the faint shout of "Fire! Fire!" from the house.

Probably one of the footmen, Earnshaw thought, casting a look over his shoulder at the thick curtain of smoke drifting across the garden, and then at Amanda as he felt her hands close around his wrists. Her fingers were cold and trembling.

"You must go," she said urgently, glancing around frantically as she drew him to his feet. "Oh, where in blazes is your horse?"

"Halfway home by now, I'm sure," the captain replied, grinning at her curse.

"Then you must flee on foot," Amanda said, and began dragging him toward the wall. "Someone will be coming from the house any moment now!"

"But, my lady, there's no need—"

"Are you insane?" She cried, whirling to face him on the lip of the slope. "How can you possibly explain your presence here? You are not one of the duchess's guests!"

She was wrong about that, but right about explaining his presence, not to mention her own. Obviously, she had yet to think of that, but he had.

"And how will my lady explain herself?"

"Don't worry, I'll—I'll think of something. Now go!"

Goaded by the clatter of footsteps on the terrace, and deciding he had enough to explain to his mother as it was, Earnshaw nodded and started for the wall. If the man under the tree was in fact her brother she'd be safe enough; if he wasn't, she'd have the devil's own time explaining herself without his presence to further complicate her predicament. He'd only taken two steps, however, when he felt a tug on his sleeve and turned back to Amanda.

"So your evening's work will not be a total waste," she said, plucking her pearl earrings from her ears and holding them out to him.

"Keep your ear bobs, my lady," Earnshaw replied, taking a step toward her. "I'll take this instead."

Gripping her small shoulders between his hands, he kissed her, very quickly but very thoroughly. And then he vaulted over the wall in the darkness.

Chapter Four

The swoon Amanda decided it was best to fall into to avoid lengthy and sticky explanations was only partially feigned. She had been kissed before, but not on the lips, never in such a shockingly familiar manner—and never by a thief.

Her mother, however, swooned so often that Amanda was able to maintain her ruse despite the heap of burgundy satin the Countess Hampton collapsed into when her father carried her through the French doors into the ballroom. The only thing that threatened to start her giggling and give her away was the Duchess of Braxton's exasperated cry, "Oh, for heaven's sake, Cornelia, not *now!*"

Once past that rough patch, however, Amanda was able to keep her eyes closed and lie limply on a settee in a downstairs saloon while the duchess dispatched a maid for the smelling salts, directed the footman carrying her mother to another settee, and Lord Hampton questioned a still groggy and mortified Andrew about Jack and Harry and Smythe. They were much too busy to notice the soft smile on her face or the fingertips she raised to trace her lips.

Her pretense held beautifully until her mother was revived and threw herself into the arms of the duchess, her lifelong friend, who sat beside her on the settee.

"Oh, Eugenia!" She sobbed. "Amanda is *ruined*! And all our wonderful plans for her future and Lesley's are *dashed*!"

"Hardly, Cornelia," the duchess soothed patiently, as she patted her on the back. "Swooning in a garden and muddying one's dress never ruined anyone."

"But you don't *understand*!" The Countess wailed tearfully. "That old dragon Matilda Blumfield noticed Amanda's absence, and while you and Andrew and dear Hampton were searching for her she demanded to know her whereabouts! She was so *dreadful*, and I was so *frightened* she'd bruit it about that Amanda had taken herself off right under my nose that I told her she'd taken a megrim and I'd sent her home with Andrew! And then—" Lady Hampton paused to sniffle and hiccup— "there she was, standing *right by* the terrace doors when dear Hampton carried her inside and—"

"Mama, how could you!" Amanda cried, shooting upright on the settee. "I've never had a megrim in my life!"

"And apparently, my gel," the duchess said with a dubiously arched eyebrow, as the countess swooned again and she lifted one of her limp hands and began to chafe it, "you've never *swooned*, either."

"But I *did*, Your Grace," Amanda insisted, crossing the fingers of one hand behind her back. *"Truly."*

The Duchess of Braxton's eyebrow slid up another doubtful notch. Her Grace, whose temper was nearly as formidable as her poise, could quite justifiably hold her at least partially responsible for making a shambles of the ball. Her green eyes were already beginning to smolder, but it occurred to Amanda suddenly that she could use the duchess's anger to her advantage.

"I did try not to," she went on earnestly, "but I don't think any young lady of sensibility would have been able *not* to swoon after such a kiss."

"Kiss!" Lord Hampton roared, abandoning his interrogation of Andrew to grasp her by the shoulders. "Which of those vile thieves *dared* touch you?"

Amanda had meant to infuriate the duchess, not her father, whose temperate nature was as remarked upon as her mother's swooning spells. Dumbstruck by his passionate and uncharacteristic response, she could do nothing but gape at him until Andrew appeared at his side.

"It was Smythe, wasn't it?" Her brother demanded.

"Heaven's no!" She cried then, her nose wrinkling in revulsion. "It was the gentleman in the black mask!"

"What gentleman in the black mask?" Lord Hampton bellowed, letting go of Amanda and wheeling on Andrew. "And where were you while some blackguard was having his way with your sister?"

"But, sir, I—"

"Say nothing." Lord Hampton held up a shaky hand, as much to control himself, thought Amanda, as to silence her brother. "I apologize for my outburst, Eugenia. We will continue this—er—discussion at home."

Frowning at Andrew, he strode across the room, opened the door—and caught the Baroness Matilda

Blumfield, the most notorious gossip among the beau monde, as she all but fell into the room. The duchess gave an indignant cry, but Amanda groaned, covered her face with her hands, and thanked God her mother had already fainted.

"If I were you, Hampton," said the short, squat baroness, as she quickly recovered her balance and her aplomb, "I'd thrash the two of them within an inch of their lives."

"Perhaps, madam," Lord Hampton retorted frostily, "Blumfield should do the same to you."

"We-e-e-ll!" The baroness gasped, every inch of her plump figure going stiff with outrage. "I have *never—*"

"Your pardon, Your Grace," the butler said, appearing in the doorway behind the baroness. "A Mr. Fisk from Bow Street is waiting to see you in the library."

"Assure him nothing was stolen, Denham," replied the duchess, who was glaring at the baroness and still holding Lady Hampton's hand, "and ask him to come back tomorrow."

"Your Grace." The butler paused and cleared his throat. "He has Master Theodore with him."

"What?" She shrieked, leaping so suddenly to her feet that she nearly jerked the countess off the settee. "Oh, Lud, what *now!*"

Dropping her friend's hand, she rushed out of the room behind Denham with the Baroness Blumfield, her beady little eyes agleam, on her heels. Lord Hampton started after them, but wheeled back to glare at his children.

"Summon the carriage, Andrew, and take your mother and sister home. I shall remain here to see if I can be assistance to Her Grace and Theodore. I will see the both of you in my study tomorrow morning, however, at ten o'clock *promptly*."

"Yes, sir," they replied in unison.

As the saloon door closed behind him, Amanda lowered her hands and turned a wide-eyed gaze on her brother. "I've really put us in the sauce this time, haven't I?"

"That you have," he agreed sourly, "and Father is going to baste us in it at ten o'clock tomorrow morning *promptly*. Whatever possessed you to tell such a wild tale?"

"It isn't a tale," Amanda retorted hotly. "There *was* a gentleman in a black mask, and he *did* kiss me!"

"I saw no such person," Andrew replied with a raised eyebrow. "There was only Jack and Harry and Smythe."

"Of course you didn't see him!" Amanda sprang angrily to her feet. "You'd already hit your head and fallen unconscious when he jumped his horse over the garden wall!"

"There was no horse, either," Andrew pointed out, his eyebrow sliding further up his forehead.

"He bolted when I jumped out of the tree!"

"And threw his rider, I suppose."

"No, I knocked him out of his saddle as I fell."

"For which, I'm sure, he was so grateful he kissed you."

"No! I offered him my earrings, but he took a kiss instead."

"Thank God you didn't tell Father that!"

"I didn't intend to tell Papa anything. I meant only to incite the duchess and make her think twice of marrying me off to Captain Earnshaw."

"Well, you botched it," Andrew stated flatly. "And if you've any sense at all, you'll confess to Father you made the whole thing up."

"But I *didn't!*"

Andrew said nothing, just raised his other eyebrow, and left the saloon to call for their carriage.

He doesn't believe me, Amanda realized, and fell back onto the settee in a daze. She tried again in the carriage on their way home to convince him, but he remained unmoved. She was so upset by his mulishness, that it didn't occur to her until she'd bathed, washed the leaves and twigs out of her hair, and sat down on the hearth rug before the fire in her room to brush it dry that her purpose would be as well served if no one—*especially* the Duchess of Braxton—believed her story of the man in the black mask.

As Andrew had pointed out, there was no physical evidence whatsoever to prove he'd been in the garden. Perhaps Her Grace would also think she'd made him up. Or even better, that she'd *imagined* him, that she was given to hysterics, that she was a goosecap, a bacon brain, and wholly unsuited to being her daughter-in-law.

And perhaps she was, Amanda reflected pensively, as she put her brush away and got into bed. How could she have let—no, helped—the man in the black mask escape? Where had her determination to capture the thieves vanished to? *Why* had it vanished? She certainly hadn't been overcome by his handsomeness because it had been dark and his mask had covered his nose and cheekbones and most of his forehead. The only one of his features she could clearly recall was his mouth; and not the shape of it so much as the feel of it.

She could feel his lips still, Amanda thought, if she concentrated hard enough, but she wasn't at all sure she ought to. The depth and intensity of the sensations that had jolted through her when he'd kissed her had both thrilled and shaken her. Nothing Andrew had told her about the ways of men and women had prepared her for it. She very much wanted to talk to her brother about it, but how could she when he didn't believe her?

Truth or fabrication would be of no concern to the Baroness Blumfield, however. The shocking story of Lady Amanda Gilbertson being kissed by a man in a black mask under the beech tree in the Duchess of Braxton's garden would be all over London by tomorrow's luncheon. But mightn't that, too, work to her advantage? If she were disgraced—and knowing the baroness's love of embellishment, Amanda had every reason to believe she would be— Her Grace would be *forced* to renege!

She might very well be banished to Hampton Hall for the rest of her life, but *anything*, Amanda told herself, even ruination and virtual imprisonment, would be preferable to marrying Lesley Earnshaw. Content that she'd managed to save herself from a fate worse than death (not quite the way she'd planned but saved nonetheless), she fell asleep with a smile on her face and her fingertips curled against her lower lip.

Her euphoria faded, however, when a footman ushered her and Andrew into their father's study at ten o'clock the next morning. Looking harried and angry, and very, *very* determined, Lord Hampton rose behind his desk.

"Sit," he commanded, indicating the two chairs set before him. Once they'd done so, he folded his hands behind him and began. "Your mother and Her Grace are, even as we speak, paying a call on the Baroness Blumfield. They hope to dissuade her from repeating your ridiculous story of the *gentleman* in the black mask."

"It's not a ridiculous story, Papa," Amanda replied. "It's the truth."

Lord Hampton glanced at Andrew.

"I saw no such person, sir," he said, shifting uncomfortably in his chair.

"Andy didn't see him," Amanda explained, "because he was unconscious when the man in the mask jumped his horse over the garden wall. I thought he was a thief, in league with Jack and Harry and Smythe, but when I knocked him out of his saddle he begged my pardon and—"

"When you *what?*" Lord Hampton's eyebrows shot up his forehead and all but disappeared into his graying fair hair.

"When I jumped out of the beech tree," Amanda continued. "I meant to land on Smythe, who was about to make off with the duchess's belongings. I couldn't allow that, of course, so I—"

"Enough!"

More startled than she'd ever been in her life (with the possible exception of the night before, when she'd jumped out of the tree and found herself sitting on a man's chest), Amanda sat blinking at her father. His face was flushed, and a wisp of his hair had fallen over his forehead. He brushed it back, took several deep breaths and reclasped his hands.

"Telling this preposterous tale will do you no good, Amanda," Lord Hampton warned. "If you thought to shock Her Grace, then have another think. She and I and your mother are still determined to have this marriage."

"But, Papa, I *loathe* Lesley Earnshaw!"

"Too late, my girl. You should have considered the possibility that I might arrange a match for you before you returned the Marquis of Claxton's poem with his spelling and grammar corrected, before you took young Deaver for twenty pounds at hazard, before you did everything you could think of to put off every young man who's shown the slightest interest in you!"

"I will *not* marry Lesley Earnshaw!" Amanda declared fiercely.

"You no longer have a choice," her father replied flatly. "Even if your mother and Her Grace are successful in dissuading the baroness, the fact remains you've come within a hair's breadth of scandal. I can no longer allow or ignore such behavior."

"You see!" Amanda shrilled, flinging herself sideways in her chair to face Andrew. "I *told* you!"

Amanda never cried, but gazing at her pale face, at the unshed tears glistening in her eyes, Lord Hampton felt his heart bump against his breastbone. He'd brought her to this with his silly pride in her accomplishments, unladylike though they were. He despised himself so thoroughly and loved his daughter so devotedly that he almost wished he could marry Lord Earnshaw himself to spare her.

"I would not marry you to an ogre, Amanda." He came around the desk, sat on one corner and took her hands in his. "You and Lesley had a few childish squabbles, but you're grown now. He did quite well at Oxford, and distinguished himself in the Peninsula and at Waterloo. Be reasonable, pet. You haven't seen the man in ten years."

"Neither have *you*, Papa," Amanda replied pointedly.

"Be that as it may." Lord Hampton frowned, loosed her hands and rose to his feet. "Consider yourself betrothed to Lord Lesley Earnshaw."

Chapter Five

Like noble blood and wealth, hazel eyes and raven hair, that tended to gray prematurely in streaks of silver at the temples, ran in the Earnshaw family. Though she was an Earnshaw by marriage only, Eugenia, the Dowager Duchess of Braxton, had such a streak in her dark hair.

Some matrons of the *ton* whispered cattily behind their fans that it was an affectation, an artful dusting of powder applied by her dresser. But it was genuine, and the cause of it, her middle son Lesley, sat smiling at Her Grace with infuriating calm in her Bond Street drawing room just after nuncheon that afternoon.

"Have you heard a single word I've said?" she demanded of him furiously.

"Every syllable, Mother," Earnshaw replied languidly from his chair opposite hers near the marble fireplace. "And I'm certain every passerby on the street has as well."

"And what is your answer?"

Feigning a look of surprise, he pressed one hand to his casually knotted cravat. "Do you *expect* one, dear?"

"Of course I expect one." Her Grace clenched her teeth and her fists in her lap to quell the urge she felt to box his ears. "I've given you a clear and simple choice."

"Sounded more to me like an ultimatum."

"Call it what you will, but choose—marriage to Amanda Gilbertson or poverty."

"I must own, Mother," Earnshaw admitted unperturbedly, as he laced his fingers over his buff waistcoat and laid his elbows on the arms of his chair, "I've always thought blackmail beneath you."

"You leave me no alternative," she informed him curtly. "It's quite bad enough that you chose last night to involve yourself in a duel, worse that you embarrassed me before the whole of the *ton* by failing to appear at the ball I hosted in *your* honor, but utterly *unforgiveable* that you embroiled Teddy, who idolizes and emulates you at every turn, in such a scandalous undertaking."

"I see." Earnshaw bent one elbow, laid the first two fingers of his hand upon his jaw and winced. There was a bruise there, which he'd noticed that morning in his shaving glass, but beyond the small twinge of pain, there was only pleasure at the recollection of the thrashing he'd taken at the hands of the delightful little minx who'd dropped upon him from the beech tree. "Would you prefer, then, that he emulate Charles?"

"I would *prefer*," Her Grace replied pointedly, "that Teddy be given an opportunity to choose the kind of man he wishes to become without any influence from *either* of his brothers."

"And you think marrying me off to the Gilbertson chit will accomplish that?"

"I think it will mark a good beginning."

There was just a hint of wistfulness in his mother's voice, a clue to Earnshaw that her temper, as fearsome and formidible as her poise, had nearly played itself out. She'd been in full cry when he'd arrived in answer to her summons, and though her report of Teddy being apprehended by Bow Street and dragged home by his ear had brought a vividly funny and richly deserved scene of humiliation to his mind, he'd had better sense than to laugh. Out loud, at least.

He'd savored it silently, chortling to himself until Her Grace had laid down her edict—marry Amanda Gilbertson or lose his income. She'd threatened him before, but never in the fullness of her anger and *never* with cutting his purse strings. Lesley had no doubt she meant it or that she'd do it. Still, he was not unduly worried, for he had the scathingly clever plan Teddy had put into his head the night before—which he'd since had time to refine—and nearly as much savoir faire as his mother.

It wouldn't serve to give in too easily, however; that would be suspicious and mightily out of character. So instead, he reached for the walking stick which was, he thought, a deft touch to the scheme aimed at forcing the Gilbertson chit to cry off, worried his thumb on the carved ivory cap and eyed his mother soberly. It was difficult, however, for a smile still played about his lips at the memory of gleaming tousled hair and eyes made luminous by firelight.

"As a gentleman and a dutiful son, I feel honor bound to point out the flaws in your reasoning," he said. "Should I refuse and you make good your threat, I could rejoin my regiment, which would at least provide me a living. Or I could appeal to Charles, who is, despite his peculiarities and vagaries, still head of the family."

"Pooh." The duchess sniffed. "On naught but a captain's salary you'd be up the River Tick within a sennight. And Charles," she finished, with a serenely smug smile, "cannot bestir himself from his library at Braxton Hall long enough to bother with such trivial concerns. He's quite content to leave such mundane matters as finances in *my* most capable hands."

This was alarming. So alarming that Lesley straightened from his studied slouch to sit bolt upright in his chair. It was one thing to allow their mother to rule in domestic affairs, but quite another to give a female, even one so sensible as Eugenia Earnshaw, control of the family capital. It simply was not done.

"What in blazes," Lesley cried, "has taken possession of Charles?"

"Roman ruins and antiquities, I believe." Her Grace shrugged dismissively. "He blathered on and on about them in his last letter to me. He is apparently quite consumed."

And so would he be, Lesley realized, in his mother's snare, if his plan to turn Amanda Gilbertson's affections failed. But it would not, for it was flawless in its simplicity, as perfectly thought out, he realized—with a burst of admiration for her cleverness—as the parson's mousetrap his mother had baited for him.

Still, it wouldn't do to give over without at least a semblance of opposition. Ergo, he surged to his feet, gasping in mid-spring, falling heavily upon his stick, and grasping the back of his left leg. Though one eyebrow notched upward a fraction, Her Grace was otherwise unmoved by the clutch of pain which he'd practiced, he'd thought to perfection, before his mirror that morning.

"Were I the eldest, I could understand your eagerness to see me wed," he declared. "Which prompts me to ask why you are actively seeking to see *me* leg shackled rather than His Dottiness?"

The duchess went rigid with renewed fury in her chair. "How *dare* you refer to your brother by that name in my presence!"

"Oh, damn and blast it, Mother!" Lesley shouted, the temper he'd inherited from his parent exploding along with hers. "According to Teddy, *everyone* calls Charles His Dottiness! This can hardly be the first you've heard it!"

"Do *not* swear in my house!" The duchess cried. "And no, it's not the first I've heard it, but I am *shocked* to hear it from your lips! And I'll thank you to keep Charles, who has nothing at all to do with anything, out of this!"

"Oh, but he *does*, Mother," Lesley countered, "for Hawksley calling Charles His Dottiness is the reason I called him out!"

The duchess's green eyes widened in surprise.

"Teddy did not tell me that."

Lesley was certain there was a great deal more Teddy hadn't told her; such as finding him at Madame Sophia's masquerade, for one, but he wouldn't betray the little scamp to their mother, even to wiggle himself off her hook. Not, of course, that Teddy didn't deserve it.

For in retrospect it had occurred to Lesley that last evening's fiasco was—indirectly, at least—all Teddy's fault. If he hadn't been at Madame's in the first place, if he hadn't insisted Lesley don that damned silly mask to hide his identity from the Runners . . . Oh, well, it was done, and the best he could hope now was that Teddy had kept mum about the particulars of his escape.

45

His mother had said nothing about the fire in the garden or discovering his bewitching little assailant under the beech tree with her so-called brother, and though Lesley longed to ask her name and direction—just out of curiosity, of course, to see if her hair really was that lustrous shade of burnished red in daylight—he didn't dare.

Much as he regretted leaving her to face certain censure, he was still convinced that admitting his presence in the garden would only complicate her predicament. He trusted his mother's silence meant she'd given a believable account of herself; still, whoever she was, she was a lady of Quality, and it was hardly an honorable thing he'd done abandoning her. He felt ashamed reliving his vault over the wall, but knew he'd already said too much in revealing the circumstances that had landed him in Regent's Park with a rapier in his hand.

Falling back on his wounded war hero pose, he rubbed at his leg and hobbled a bit as he reseated himself. His mother, he noted, remained nonplussed.

"If you must know," she said, her composure recollected, "I've quite given up on Charles. I've worn myself thin throwing marriageable young ladies at his head to no avail. He is three and thirty, and quite hopelessly confirmed, I'm convinced, in crusty bachelorhood. How I raised such a reclusive and scholarly son I can't think, other than to own I somehow failed miserably in his upbringing."

"Fustian, Mother," Lesley said mildly. "You've never given up on anything. You quite reformed our father, who was the Terror of the *Ton* until you set your cap for him and tamed him."

"I was young then," she replied, "young enough to believe anything was possible, but age has since taught me otherwise. I've neither the time nor the patience to reform Charles. I'm tired, Lesley. I *long* for my dower house with its rose garden and little village closeby." Her Grace sighed heavily, then fixed a determined look on him. "I'm also sick to death of hearing my eldest son called His Dottiness, Teddy referred to as a Master Jacaanapes, and *you* hailed far and wide as a rakehell."

This, too, was Fustian, and Lesley wasn't fooled by it. His mother, who thrived on the frantic pace of London, would go mad within a fortnight surrounded by roses and country squires.

"Captain Rakehell," he pronounced, his voice slow and bemusedly thoughtful. "Has rather a nice ring to it, don't you think?"

The duchess again stiffened in her chair.

"Does that mean you've made your choice?"

"No, dear, it does not," he sighed, deciding the time had come to capitulate. "I really have no choice, do I? I was merely daydreaming aloud."

A brilliant smile of triumph lit his mother's face.

"A wise decision," she pronounced approvingly, "one which assures me that you are, thank God, more sensible than your behavior last night might otherwise indicate."

"Yes, well," Lesley replied uncomfortably, again reminded of his ungentlemanly conduct. "I wouldn't congratulate myself on total victory just yet, if I were you. Though you have me flanked and my supply line cut, the enemy has yet to accept your terms."

"The enemy?" Her Grace queried, trying to look puzzled but not quite managing it. "I wish you wouldn't use military terms, Lesley, for you know I've no head for war."

"Fustian, Mother," he said again. "You're a consummate strategist. Had you been born a man,

I'm certain you would have been at the Duke's right hand at Waterloo."

"If you're referring to the Lady Amanda," the duchess replied, raising an eyebrow but otherwise letting his comment pass, "then I can assure you your proposal will be accepted."

"Are you so certain? Have neither you or Lord Hampton considered the possibility that his daughter and I may simply not suit?"

"Of course you will suit," Her Grace retorted swiftly. "Why wouldn't you? You've known each other all your lives, and Amanda holds you in great affection."

Bloody hell, swore Lesley under his breath, closely watching his mother's face for a sign of hesitancy or doubt. But there was none, not the tiniest qualm in her voice or expression. Teddy had apparently told the truth, he thought, and decided—without pausing to consider that his mother was as gifted a teller of half-truths as he—that he would have to lay it on very thick indeed with the Gilbertson chit.

"Well, yes, that's true," he granted with another sigh. "I reckon we can manage to deal together well enough. So long as you don't expect me to act the devoted husband."

"That's not a question you should ask of me," Her Grace replied with a twinkling and knowing half smile, "but rather of Amanda."

"I suppose so," Lesley agreed glumly, and got stiffly to his feet. "Very well, Mother. You may summon the hangman."

"I beg your pardon?"

"So sorry. I meant to say send a notice to the *Times.*"

Her Grace laughed gaily, the shining smile on her still lovely face. Though her obvious relish of her victory pricked Lesley's pride, he knew her triumph would be brief, and so chose to let her enjoy it while she could.

"You are merely being married," she said, "not murdered."

"Is there a difference?"

"Just like your father." Her Grace *tsk*ed at him fondly, then grew thoughtful. "Lady Cottingham's ball is two days hence. I shall, of course, expect you to escort Amanda. And you will, in the interim, have ample time to present yourself to her and to Lord Hampton."

"As Your Grace wishes." Bracing himself on his cane, Lesley gave her a small bow, and accepted the hand she lifted to him.

As he touched his lips to her smooth knuckles, his mother surprised him by disengaging her fingers from his and cupping his bruised jaw in her palm. He winced again, but she didn't seem to notice.

"You've made me very happy, Lesley," she said, gently stroking the curve of his cheek.

"I'm glad, Mother." He caught her hand, kissed her fingertips, and straightened. "Now if you'll excuse me, I'm expected at White's."

His mother nodded, and he left, limping markedly on his left leg. Once the door had closed behind him, the duchess was out of her chair in a flash and at the window that faced Bond Street. She lifted the drape and peeped out, just as Lesley reached the flagway and strode—briskly and rather purposefully, thought Her Grace—toward his waiting carriage, the cane he had leaned so heavily upon only moments before swinging loosely from his hand.

"Oh, you wicked, *wicked* boy," she laughed softly, and let the drape fall.

Chapter Six

Despite the heavy midafternoon traffic, which made for slow going and frequent stops between Bond Street and his Mayfair establishment, the normally impatient Captain Lord Lesley Earnshaw reclined contentedly against the blue velvet squabs of his carriage.

"Captain Rakehell," he murmured, grinning as he recalled the angry flush the name had brought to his mother's cheeks.

She was a dear, really. Scheming, conniving and dictatorial, but a dear nonetheless, and he adored her. Not enough to marry Amanda Gilbertson to please her, but that was part of the fun.

And to think he'd worried civilian life would be stiflingly dull. Why, he'd scarce been home a fortnight, had already fought a duel (at least part of one), and was now up to his shirt points in intrigue. What more could one ask?

The well-sprung barouche jolted to a sudden halt just then, pitching him head first toward the opposite banquette. By quickly throwing up one leg—his left, unthinkingly, and wincing as a stab of genuine pain shot through the muscles—Lesley caught himself and saved his chin a nasty scraping on the squabs. Muttering a curse, he grasped the edge of the lowered window, levered himself out of it and craned his head toward the box.

"Have a care, Ruston!" he shouted.

"Sorry, m'lord!" his driver returned. "But some bloody fool jus' cut 'is team right in front of—'Ere, *you*!" The coachman broke off and grabbed his whip. "You can't—"

The right hand door sprang open and a small man dressed in gray city clothes climbed into the carriage and seated himself opposite Lesley, who was still hanging out the window. Planting the walking stick he carried between his knees, he folded his hands on top of it, nodded, and said, quite conversationally, "Good afternoon, Lord Earnshaw."

Wishing he had his rapier or a pistol, or at least his cane, which lay out of his reach on the banquette, Lesley eyed the intruder balefully, swung himself back inside and observed forcefully, "Cut purses have certainly grown bold in my absence."

The man's laugh was interrupted by the appearance of the bewhiskered Ruston, brandishing his whip, and the groom Tom, his fists doubled and his square jaw clenched, in the still open carriage door.

"A moment, if you please." The man held up a hand to them, reached inside his coat, and produced a card, which he handed to Lesley.

He scanned it quickly, then eyed the intruder again, this time incredulously. "Bow Street! What is the meaning of this?"

"If you would instruct your men to carry on, my lord—" the Runner paused to glance significantly at Ruston and Tom "—all will be explained by the time we reach Mayfair."

He could, of course, have the man—Mr. Gerald Fisk, according to his card—summarily tossed into the gutter, but his curiosity was piqued. "Very well," Lesley acquiesced. "Get us under way, Ruston."

"Can't, m'lord. Our way be blocked."

"If you will remount your box, coachman," Fisk told him, "my associate will remove our carriage from your path and follow at a discreet distance."

Ruston frowned suspiciously and glanced at Lord Earnshaw. He nodded, and the two servants withdrew, closing the door behind them.

"Are the methods employed by Bow Street always this unorthodox?" Lesley asked, slipping the card into his inside pocket.

"Rarely, my lord." Fisk smiled and refolded his hands atop his cane as the barouche rolled forward. "But because the matter I wish to discuss with you will require a good deal of discretion, I felt the means justified. In the excitement of our near collision I doubt anyone noticed me slipping into your coach."

"For the sake of discretion you risked life and limb? Not to mention my cattle?"

"There was very little risk." He shrugged dismissively. "My associate is quite a skilled driver."

"You are aware that I will verify your credentials?"

"Of course. If you don't, my lord, I'll be forced to reassess your character."

Satisfied, at least for the moment, that Fisk was who and what he said he was, Lesley settled back against the banquette.

"Now what is this discreet matter you wish to discuss?"

"The robbery—or rather, the attempt at robbery—that was made last evening at your mother's home."

"I cannot help you, for I was not on the premises at the time."

"Were you not, my lord?" Fisk smiled and leaned forward on his cane. "In questioning Her Grace's guests—in particular the Baroness Matilda Blumfield—I heard a most preposterous story regarding a man in a black mask."

"Really?" Lesley rejoined lazily, covering the jolt of surprise he'd just been given with a feigned yawn. "One of the thieves, I'm sure."

"Are you, my lord?"

"Am I what?"

"Are you *sure* it was one of the thieves?"

"Of course I'm not sure. How could I be, since I've just told you I was *not* at my mother's house last night."

"How odd." Fisk pursed his lips perplexedly. "I could have sworn your younger brother Theodore told me he'd arranged to meet you with fresh clothing in the stables."

Lesley laughed, though it sounded a bit forced even to him. "What a prankster our Teddy is."

"So I've been told." Fisk smiled, not altogether pleasantly. "But I can assure you, my lord, he wasn't in a jesting mood last night when I accompanied him home from Regent's Park."

"Good heavens!" Lesley did his best to look shocked, despite the strong feeling he had that his ploy of ignorance wasn't working. "Whatever was he doing there?"

The smile vanished from the Bow Street Runner's face.

"May I suggest, my lord, that you leave off trying to bam me so we may get down to cases?"

His ruse definitely wasn't working, still Lesley stiffened indignantly on the banquette. "Now see here, Fisk—"

"Your brother confessed everything to me," he interrupted. "The duel, the mask you took from him at the Cyprian masquerade, *everything*, my lord. I paid a call on Sir Alex Hawksley this morning, and no more believe his valet dropped the razor while shaving him and cut his shoulder than I believe that you were *not* in your mother's garden last night at more or less the same time as the thieves, because the sack of items they attempted to make off with was found near the wall, where the ground is muddy and full of hoofprints."

A good portion of successful soldiering—and Captain Lord Earnshaw had been a very good soldier, indeed—was recognizing when the odds were against you and you were about to be overwhelmed.

"If you wished merely to question me about the robbery," he replied, striving to change tactics, "why didn't you call upon me at my home?"

Fisk's small, narrow face took on a sly look, not a smile so much as a subtle lifting of the lines around his calculating gray eyes.

"Obviously, my lord, that's not what I want."

"Then what *do* you want?"

"Your help in apprehending the thieves."

Lesley laughed again, this time genuinely. "You can't be serious!"

"I'm prepared to drop all charges stemming from the duel you fought last evening," Fisk explained brusquely, "in exchange for your assistance. Should you decline, however, I will have no choice but to prosecute."

"Outrageous!" Lesley cried angrily. "That's blackmail!"

"I prefer to call it persuasion," Fisk corrected, "though from your point of view it would also be certain social ruin, for I would also, naturally, have to bring charges against Sir Alex Hawksley."

"Oh, naturally," Lesley agreed caustically. "And how much damage, do you suppose, will be done to my reputation if it gets out I've actually stooped to helping enforce the law? Or do you even care?"

"Under the circumstances, not especially, my lord," he admitted, "for you did clearly and willfully violate the law. However, if you are discreet, and rely upon the mask you took from your brother, the part you play in the arrest need never become public knowledge."

"What has that cursed and damned mask to do with this?"

"Everything, my lord, for it is the beauty of the plan." Fisk leaned eagerly forward, his expression animated.

God help me, Lesley moaned silently, another plan.

"Allow me to explain further. The mode of operation employed by these thieves is for one of the band to take the place of a servant. After each robbery, tied and gagged footmen stripped of their livery have been found in some part of the house or grounds. Their method is quite brilliant, for ladies and gentlemen of Quality accord servants and furniture equal notice."

The observation stung, but its veracity couldn't be denied, not even by Lesley, who'd himself been guilty of such haughtiness before enlisting in the Second. His experiences on Spanish battlefields, however, had taught him that nobility and honor were determined by more than the circumstances of one's birth.

"They strike only at Society affairs, balls, routs, and the like," Fisk continued, "and as best we can deduce, during the supper hour. With the guests at table, the thief is then relatively free to help himself to whatever valuables he's had time to reconnoiter."

"It's a clever scheme," Lesley granted. "But having reasoned it out, why does Bow Street need me? Why don't you plant a few of your number among the guests?"

"We've done that, my lord, to no avail," Fisk replied, a hint of chagrin in his voice. "Apparently, we stick out like bandaged thumbs, and we have been forced to conclude that anyone can masquerade as a footman, but only a gentleman can play the part of a gentleman."

"I'm sure that's true," Lesley agreed, only a bit smugly, "but why, then, don't you pass yourselves off as footmen?"

"That, too, has been considered, but for two reasons discarded. One, Bow Street lacks sufficient manpower to infiltrate the staff of every Society establishment in London, and second, there is a great pressure being applied to apprehend these thieves. A close friend of the Regent, robbed of over ten thousand pounds in objects d'art, made appeal to His Highness, who has taken an interest in the matter."

"Poor fellow." Lesley *tsk*ed piteously, an amused smile tugging at his lips. "You *are* in a coil."

"A bit of one, yes," Fisk granted, smiling back at him. "But then, my lord, so are *you*."

"Yes, well." Lesley frowned sourly. "We are nearing Mayfair, and you've yet to say precisely what it is you want me to do."

"I want you to appear again as the gentleman in the black mask."

"To what end?"

"To this end, my lord." Fisk hunched more eagerly over his cane. "Based on the Baroness Blumfield's reputation, I'm certain the story of the man in the black mask will have spread all over London by evening. Her ladyship is convinced he's the thief who attempted last night's robbery."

It hadn't occurred to Lesley to wonder how the old dragon had heard the tale when Fisk had mentioned her earlier, but he did now. Was the connection his mind instantly made between the baroness, the bruise on his cheek, and the little minx who'd put it there—who had also believed him a thief—as logical as it seemed?

"Did the old besom happen to say how she came to hear the story?"

"No, my lord, she didn't," Fisk replied, stifling a grin, "for we were interrupted at that point by morning callers."

"I should very much like to know how she heard of him," Lesley said, frowning thoughtfully.

"I intend to question the baroness again and will ask her. Now." Fisk glanced out the window to check their progress, then continued. "There is among thieves a degree of professional courtesy. Simply, one does not poach on another's territory; to do so would be considered a serious breach. And here, my lord, is where you enter in. If the thieves hear of the man in the black mask, and thanks to the Baroness Blumfield and her tongue they surely will, and are given to believe he's encroaching upon their preserve—"

"Good God!" Lesley exploded, so suddenly that

Fisk started and nearly dropped his cane. "You intend to use me as bait for your hook!"

"Not in the sense of being swallowed by the fish," Fisk corrected hurriedly, "but merely as a lure, my lord, an enticement to draw them out."

"And what if it does? Draw them out, I mean? Where will you be?"

"Near enough at hand to lend whatever assistance may be required."

Folding his arms, Lesley eyed the smallish, narrow-framed Runner dubiously. "Forgive my plain speaking, Fisk, but that's not a great deal of comfort."

"Appearances sometimes deceive, my lord," he replied without umbrage. "And I shouldn't worry if I were you. As neatly as you took Sir Alex, I doubt that a lone thief will cause you much trouble."

"A moment ago we were dealing with *thieves*."

"Oh, we are, my lord, for definitely the man on the inside has outside accomplices, but we have only to apprehend *one*." Fisk smiled as the barouche slowed to negotiate a corner. "There may be professional courtesy, my lord, but there is no honor among thieves. Whichever one we catch up will not wish to go alone to Newgate and will be most eager to give us the names and direction of his cohorts."

It occurred to Lesley that being himself taken up by Bow Street would certainly rid him of Amanda Gilbertson, but he'd never fancied the notion of emigration. And there was the surety that if charges were brought against him, Teddy would be caught up as well, at least as witness, and he had even less desire to live out his days a pauper.

"I clearly have no choice but to assist you, Fisk—as obviously you've been aware all along—but I do have one or two questions. How long will I be expected to ride about in the dead of night rattling my rapier? And, by the by, I trust that's all you will require of me?"

"That's all, my lord," Fisk assured him, "and I wouldn't think it will take longer than a few days, perhaps a fortnight at best, to bring these thieves to heel."

A fortnight, at best, was the same amount of time Lesley had gauged it would take him to force the Gilbertson chit to cry off. This additional demand on his person would leave little time for White's or Jackson's, or wooing the new mistress he'd been thinking of acquiring, but better to sacrifice fourteen nights than the rest of his life.

"Very well, Fisk. Look for the gentleman in the black mask to appear at Lady Cottingham's ball."

"I shall be there as well, my lord, though, of course, you will not see me."

"Just make sure the thieves, should they put in an appearance, do not see you."

"Rest assured, my lord, they will not."

He wouldn't rest assured about anything, Lesley thought sourly as the barouche came to a stop in front of his house, until he'd rid himself of Lady Amanda Gilbertson and Mr. Gerald Fisk.

"Until then." He nodded curtly, taking up his cane and moving toward the door as Tom appeared to open it.

"Instruct your coachman to drive round to the stables," Fisk said. "My associate will pick me up there."

Lesley disembarked, relayed the message to Ruston as he crossed the flagway, and started up the steps to his house. He was limping a bit, his leg made stiff by catching himself on the banquette, and had reached the third stair when the paneled, brass-fitted doors burst inward. Teddy, his face flushed and anxious, appeared between them. He took in the ivory-capped stick, his brother's faltering gait, and went pale.

"Gemini!" He gasped. "Mother lamed you even worse! She said she meant to thrash you to within an inch of your life, but I never imagined—"

"Stow it," Lesley snapped, mounting the last two steps and brushing past him into the foyer. "She thrashed me with her tongue, you clunch, not a birch rod. The cane is but a prop," he explained, handing it along with his hat to a footman.

"But you're limping!"

"Yes, I know. Silly of me, isn't it?" Lesley cocked a sardonic eyebrow at his little brother. "Now and then I just can't seem to keep myself from it. Mayhap it has to do with the French musket ball I took in the—" He caught himself, mindful of the footman, and merely growled, "Never mind why I'm limping. What are you doing here? You and your playmates Smithers and Forbes are supposed to be on your collective way back to school."

"I sent them ahead, for I couldn't leave without begging your forgiveness and giving you an opportunity to ring a peal over my head." Teddy gripped the newel post of the curved stairway with both hands and braced himself. "I'm ready whenever you are."

"Leave off, wretched halfling." Lesley rumpled his hair, a grudging smile replacing his frown as he moved past him and up the stairs. "I wager you've suffered enough at the hands of mother and Mr. Fisk."

"Fisk! That *cad*!" Teddy pushed himself off the post and bolted up the steps behind him. "I shall call him out myself! He swore if I told him everything he wouldn't make trouble for you!"

So that's how it is, Lesley thought sourly, turning on a carpeted step to plant a firm index finger in Teddy's neckcloth.

"You'll do no such thing. You'll take yourself back to school and let *me* deal with Mr. Gerald Fisk."

"But, Lesley, this is all my fault!"

"Indeed it is, but having yourself carted off to gaol for demanding a Bow Street Runner name his seconds will do nothing to absolve you. It would only—although it seems impossible just at the moment—make things worse."

"I suppose you're right," Teddy granted slowly, a thoughtful frown puckering his brow.

"And wipe that look off your face. I've had a belly full of schemes and plots, thank you."

With Teddy on his heels, Lesley climbed the rest of the stairs and traversed the upstairs corridor.

"Packston!" he called, turning through the doorway into his bedchamber, where his harried-looking valet was woefully regarding the garments laid out on the counterpane. "Good man." Lesley smiled expansively. "I see you've done with the shopping."

"Yes, my lord." Suppressing a shudder, Packston looked away from the horrid wardrobe laid upon the four poster. "Your tailor will arrive shortly to make the necessary fittings."

"Excellent." Lesley picked up the quizzing glass that had been at the top of the list he'd given Packston that morning and gazed archly through it at Teddy. "Do you think this will make Amanda Gilbertson swoon?"

"Dead away," Teddy assured him, gazing slack-jawed at the wildly patterned waistcoats strewn upon the bed.

"And this, sprig." Lesley snatched one up and held it to his chest. "Will I look the handsomest, bravest cove that ever lived in this?"

"No!" he cried, appalled. "You'll look the veriest fop! Or worse you'll look—" Speech failed him then, but comprehension dawned. "Oh, Lesley. You *are* clever," he said admiringly as he began to laugh.

Teddy laughed, in fact, all the long way back to his school in the Midlands.

Chapter Seven

Lord Hampton was a happy man. With the morning papers spread on his knee, seated in his favorite chair by the fire in his study, he sipped his after luncheon coffee and smiled.

Amanda had come sweet and sunny to the breakfast table, all traces of the tears and sulks of the day before vanished with the dew. Cheerfully she had gone with her mother to pay morning calls, an obligation she loathed and found odiously boring, and upon her return, had smiled at the receipt of Lord Earnshaw's note inviting her to drive with him this afternoon.

Presently, she was closeted with Lady Hampton and her abigail, selecting the perfect gown to wear, dressing her hair—for Lord Earnshaw would arrive within the half hour—and behaving as a proper female should.

Disaster with the Blumfield creature had been averted. Just how, Lord Hampton had been unable to ascertain from his wife, who'd been quite overwrought (understandably) during the interview, and afterward quite vague (characteristically) about the details.

But a thoughtful note from Eugenia Earnshaw (who knew Cornelia as well as he) had divulged the particulars: so long as she omitted the fact he'd kissed Amanda, the old dragon could gossip freely about the gentleman in the black mask; in exchange, the duchess swore to tell no one the baroness had been caught eavesdropping at the saloon door.

Skillful as Her Grace's handling of the crisis was, it would have been totally unnecessary if only she and Cornelia had consulted him in the first place. Lord Hampton would have advised them not to breathe a word about young Earnshaw to Amanda, simply to introduce them and leave the rest to Fate; or perhaps to Nature.

They were birds of a feather, his daughter and Eugenia's in-between son, both headstrong and without caution. He agreed with his wife and Her Grace that they were eminently suited to one another, but he wouldn't have said so.

Nor would he have voiced his wish to see the Earnshaw and Gilbertson families united by marriage. And the absolute last thing on earth he would have done was declare to Amanda and Earnshaw— as Cornelia had told him the duchess had done in a letter sent to him in Brussels shortly after news of his wounding at Waterloo had arrived—that the two of them had been elected by their parents to consummate (so to speak) such a union.

Despite their initial mishandling of the affair, the two ladies had, as cats always do, landed on their feet. Though a bit chagrined that they'd pulled it off, Lord Hampton was, more than anything else, relieved that it was all water under the bridge and that peace had been restored to his household.

Sighing contentedly, he raised his cup to take another sip. But as the rim touched his lips, a blood-curdling shriek from upstairs caused him to fling it from his hand. The steaming coffee which splashed down his shirtfront did as much as the scream to propel him from his chair and up the steps, scattering sheets of newsprint in his wake.

"Bennett!" Lady Hampton wailed from Amanda's bedchamber. *"Bennett!"*

She cried out for him a third time as he came through the door, his heart pounding with exertion and his neckcloth dripping, to find his wife and the abigail Marie standing over Amanda, who was still in her wrapper and seated at her dressing table. Blackened bits of something were sprinkled among the crystal vials and jars, and Amanda's eyes glittered defiantly at him in the chevral glass.

"Oh, Bennett!" The countess wailed, her body beginning to sway and her eyelids to flutter at the sight of him.

"Cornelia, don't even *think* to swoon!" Lord Hampton threatened, leaping too late across the room to prevent her collapsing in a billow of skirts at the foot of Amanda's bed. He looked helplessly at her prostrate form for a moment, then wheeled on his daughter. "What is the meaning of this?"

Raising her chin and folding her arms, Amanda compressed her lips into a hard, stubborn line and refused to answer.

"Marie?" Lord Hampton queried of the plump, apple cheeked abigail. "What do you know of this?"

"Best see f'yourself, m'lord," she replied grimly, and took a firm hold on her spirited little mistress.

But other than to grimace and close her eyes,

Amanda struggled not at all as Marie peeled back her upper lip to reveal blackened gaps in her perfect white teeth.

"What *is* that?" Lord Hampton cried.

"Harcargh," Amanda said.

"Marie, if you please."

The maid took her hand away. "Sorry m'lord."

"Again?"

"Charcoal," Amanda repeated.

"And the purpose?" Lord Hampton demanded, striving to keep his temper in check.

"To make myself look the veriest hag!" She declared, turning on her bench to glare at him proudly.

"Scrub it off this *instant*, and finish dressing to receive Lord Earnshaw! Marie, don't leave her alone for so much as one *second*!" He leveled his index finger at Amanda, then bent to collect his wife. "Once I've seen to your mother, I'll send a footman to clean out the grate!"

Puffing a bit, he turned away with Lady Hampton dangling from his arms, and Marie scooting ahead of him to hold the door open. She closed it behind him and frowned disapprovingly over her shoulder.

"Told you it wouldn't work," she said.

"Drat! And it was ever so hard to make it stick!" Turning again on the bench, Amanda bared her teeth to admire her handiwork in the glass, then made a face. "But it tastes vile."

"I shouldn't wonder," Marie replied without sympathy. "Best scrape it off and rinse your mouth."

"Poor Mama." Amanda sighed and got up from her table. "I'm a trial to her, I know, although I vow I don't mean to be."

"That you are," Marie agreed, then shook her head and clucked her tongue against the roof of her mouth. "It's a wonder her ladyship don't hurt herself hittin' the floor ten times a day."

"Not to worry," Amanda laughed. "Mama swoons so often, I'm sure she knows precisely how to fall and *not* hurt herself."

Though why she'd want to Amanda couldn't fathom, other than to own it sometimes was, as it had proven to be in the Duchess of Braxton's garden, a most effective method of escape. Hmmm, she thought, as she moved toward the washbasin, perhaps swooning was an art she'd have to perfect. What, she wondered with a grin, would happen if she fainted dead away at the sight of Lesley Earnshaw?

At that moment, Lord Hampton, having entrusted his wife to her abigail and hastily repaired his toilette, was standing speechless in the parlor, facing Captain Lord Earnshaw and wondering the very same thing.

"My dear Lord Hampton," he said, offering his beringed hand at an angle that made the earl wonder if he meant it to be clasped or kissed. "How very nice to see you after such a long time."

"So good of you to call upon Amanda," Lord Hampton replied numbly, making quick work of the handshake. "May I offer you a brandy while you wait?"

"A sherry or ratafia, perhaps," replied Lesley with a sniff. "I find that stronger spirits so early in the day invariably leave me with the headache."

Lord Hampton felt his temples begin to thud.

"But of course. If you please." He indicated a chair with a distracted wave, and all but fled to the drinks tray set on a cherry sideboard.

His hands shook as he uncapped a decanter of ratafia and filled a crystal goblet. He poured himself a brandy, eyed it a moment, then downed it, poured another, and drew a deep breath before lifting the glasses and turning to face his guest. But the smile he forced crumbled at the sight of Lord Earnshaw brushing a handkerchief deeply edged with lace over a cut velvet chair with an excessively fastidious flick of his wrist.

"Your pardon, my lord. A soldier's habit." Lesley bowed to hide the grin spreading across his face at the earl's stricken expression. "Battlefields aren't the tidiest of places. One must always look before one sits."

"Oh, but—*of course!*" Lord Hampton fairly gushed.

After the hardships and deprivations of war the lad was doing things up just a bit too brown, that was all, which explained his shirt points, the froth in his cravat, and the multitude of fobs dangling from his vividly patterned waistcoat. Reassured, he came forward with the drinks, as Lesley, grimacing and leaning heavily upon his cane, sat down.

"Ahh, much better." He again employed the lace handkerchief to mop his brow. "I'm fine once I'm up or down, but the in between plagues me still."

"How bothersome," Lord Hampton sympathized, and handed him the goblet of ratafia.

"It will pass with time, the surgeons say." Lesley set his drink on a small table and shrugged, waiting until the earl had taken the chair next to his and had raised his snifter before adding, "They further assure me the injury will have no effect on my ability to produce an heir."

The remark caught Lord Hampton in the act of swallowing. His eyes bulged, as did the tendons in his neck, but he managed to fight the brandy down before the coughing and spluttering overtook him. Solicitously, Lesley sprang to his feet to thump him on the back, forgetting to use his cane and thanking God Lord Hampton was too deeply in the throes of choking half to death to notice.

"Down the wrong pipe, eh, my lord?"

With a twinge of guilt, Lesley noted the poor man could only gasp and nod, his eyes streaming tears, and his face turning an alarming shade of purple.

"Just breathe deeply, my lord, and the spasm will pass."

It did so at last, and when Lord Hampton could draw a steady breath, he leaned his head back and closed his eyes, giving Lesley the moment he needed to nip into his chair.

"I beg pardon for my blunt speech," he said, once Lord Hampton opened his watery eyes. "I thought merely to relieve any concerns you might have before Amanda joins us."

"How thoughtful of you," Lord Hampton replied weakly, wiping his eyes with his handkerchief, and wondering if he'd acted too hastily in sending the notice of his daughter's betrothal to *The Times*.

Chapter Eight

Standing dumbstruck with disbelief, and as yet un-
seen in the parlor doorway, Amanda wished she,
too, could weep. Surely the ridiculous fop seated
with her father couldn't be Lesley Earnshaw, for
he bore no more resemblance to the rough and tumble boy she remembered than she did to the Baroness Blumfield.

His blue superfine coat and buff pantaloons
served well enough, but the pattern of his ruby
waistcoat was better suited to a drapery, and she
was certain if he turned his head too suddenly his
incredible shirt points would lop off an ear. His cravat foamed with more lace than her petticoats, his
dark hair with more curls than her own, and the
gold tassles on his Hessians would look far better
on the end of a bellpull.

"Ah, there you are, Amanda." Lord Hampton
took note of her in the doorway and rose from his
chair. "Come here, pet."

Yes, she'd swoon, and she wouldn't have to pre-
tend, Amanda decided, coming slowly forward at
her father's summons. Lord Earnshaw also came to

his feet, levering himself up with an ebony walking stick while raising—oh, heaven help her!—*a quizzing glass*!

Which masked, Lesley fervently hoped, the incredulous leap his eyelids took. The glass also warped the image of the girl moving haltingly into the room, but her face had already been indelibly etched in his mind by firelight and moonglow. The realization that he'd schemed and shammed himself into one hell of a prickly fix chased through his head, but couldn't dim the sheer delight he felt at discovering, in so unlikely a guise, the little minx who'd dropped into his life and his dreams two nights ago.

"Here we are." Lord Hampton slipped one arm around his daughter's shoulders as she stopped beside him.

"Good afternoon, Lord Earnshaw." Amanda made the small, polite curtsey expected of her and offered her hand. "How kind of you to invite me to drive with you."

There was no warmth in her eyes—the deep blue, near-violet eyes that had haunted his sleep—or in her fingertips as he bowed and drew them to his lips. Something is sorely amiss here, thought Lesley, abandoning the glass as he straightened to better gauge the depths of the ice in her gaze.

"Do call me Lesley," he replied, keeping a loose hold on her fingers. "May I say, my dear Amanda, how very lovely you've grown up to be."

"Only if I may say the same of you," she retorted, biting the tip of her tongue to stifle the "Ouch!" that sprang to her lips as her father pinched her arm.

There was defiance in the sharp glance she shot her parent, and a moment later, as her gaze raked

71

Lesley from head to foot, pure revulsion. Oh, this is famous, he realized, she *loathes* me!

He realized, too, that Teddy had lied to him, that he'd donned this ridiculous rig for naught, but couldn't muster himself to anger. Teddy deserved—and would receive—throttling for spinning this particular Banbury Tale, but at the moment, the situation was too ironic to be anything but hilarious.

Lightly, and in keeping with his character, Lesley laughed. "I do *so* admire a sense of humor."

"Obviously, my lord." Amanda withdrew her hand and again took stock of him, this time with a distastefully arched brow.

It was the look more than the comment that nicked Lesley's ego. The little adder, he thought, torn between amusement and irritation. With such a tongue, no wonder she is still unwed. What was it the Runner, Fisk, had said to him? Appearances sometimes deceive, that was it. And didn't they just, for he was no more the fop he now appeared than he was, in the guise of the gentleman in the black mask, a thief.

Perhaps, he thought, it was time Lady Amanda Gilbertson learned you cannot judge a man by the color of his waistcoat or the amount of lace on his cravat. And who better to teach her, he decided, than Captain Rakehell?

"With your permission, my lord," Lesley said, inclining his chin to hide the wicked smile curving his mouth. "We don't want to miss the height of the promenade."

"Naturally not," Lord Hampton agreed, somewhat pensively. "Do run along and enjoy yourselves."

This is the perfect moment to swoon, Amanda decided, but got no farther than the thought. For when she did not instantly take his offered arm, Lesley firmly grasped her hand, tucked and held it through the curve of his elbow, and all but dragged her out of the parlor.

Startled, and surprised at the strength in his grip, Amanda failed to notice that Lord Earnshaw forgot to use his cane. He remembered it once he'd claimed his hat from the footman in the foyer, cursed himself under his breath, and slowed their pace to lean upon it as they downed the outside steps and crossed the flagway to his curricle.

The groom Tom, holding Lord Earnshaw's splendid blacks, looked away at their approach to hide the grin on his face. Poor man, Amanda sympathized, he's as mortified as I am at being seen in the company of such a popinjay. Wishing her hat had a veil, a very *heavy* veil, she allowed herself to be handed up onto the red leather seat, smoothed her skirts, and folded her gloved hands upon her reticule, but made no effort to hide the consternation on her face.

Amused as he was by her expression, Lesley wasn't concerned about public ridicule. His curled beaver hid most of his overdone Titus, and the quick buttoning of his coat hid the dreadful waistcoat. He'd further taken the precaution of warning his most intimate cronies what he was up to, and intended to dawdle along the way to miss the zenith of the daily crush in Hyde Park.

Still . . . Amanda looked so woebegone and so charming in her blue walking dress and matching hat cocked at a jaunty angle. Her hair was as lustrously rich and red as he remembered, now pinned in coils at the nape of her neck with curls at her ears that brushed her fur-trimmed collar.

Perhaps he was being too mean, Lesley considered, all but done in by the memory of her hair loosened and tangled with leaves. Climbing into the curricle beside her, he eased himself onto the cushion he'd affected along with his costume, took the ribbons from Tom, turned to Amanda with parted lips to confess his charade, but pressed them suddenly and firmly shut.

"You're sitting on a *pillow*!" she gasped, her voice as horrified as her expression.

"Why yes," he replied, all thoughts of mercy vanishing. "Leather is so *chilly* this time of year. Would you care to share it with me?"

"Thank you, *no*." Amanda wrinkled her nose and moved primly to put the length of the seat between them.

"As you wish." Lesley shrugged, did a bit of deliberate fumbling with the leathers, then raised his hands and clucked to his team.

He wouldn't dare such a trick with any cattle but his blacks, gelded half brothers to Lucifer and gentled to harness by Lesley himself. Confused by the signal, they laid back their ears and snorted. He gave the ribbons another shake and clucked again. The blacks snorted again, stamped their hooves and backed against their traces, but still refused to budge.

"You have the leads crossed," Amanda said, patronizingly, as if speaking to a child. "Your horses won't move because you are telling them to turn into each other."

"Oh, *pooh*!" Lesley straightened the ribbons and turned on the seat to glare at Tom. "You *promised* to tell me the next time I got them crossed!"

"S-sorry, m'lord." Tom cupped one hand over his mouth to muffle the laughter making his shoulders shake.

"Do I have them right now?" Lesley asked of Amanda.

Her reply was a quizzically arched brow. "I thought you were a cavalry officer, my lord."

"Lesley," he corrected her. "And yes, I was. What of it?"

"I don't understand how you could confuse the leads."

"Don't you? When one rides there are only two to contend with. Presently, you'll note, there are four." He raised the leathers for emphasis, forcing a stiff tone into his voice. "Seems simple enough to me."

"I can see how it would," Amanda agreed, her eyebrow sliding upward another notch.

She was mocking him again, and rather expertly, too, the smile tugging at the corners of her mouth revealing her even teeth and the pink tip of her tongue. It wasn't forked, but should be, thought Lesley, glowering as he signaled to the blacks through the ribbons and eased them away from the gutter.

The humor in the situation was rapidly fading, and with it, Lesley's amusement. The pillow was the closest he'd come to knocking her off her pins, and even then she'd recovered herself with amazing quickness. He'd been right to think he'd have to lay it on very thick indeed with Lady Amanda Gilbertson. His forehead furrowed as he strove to connive a new strategy, but he realized suddenly, with a sharp intake of breath, that there was no need.

What in blazes was he thinking? This was no lisping, simpering deb, but the fiesty little vixen who'd hurled herself out of a tree and bruised his jaw! She had spirit and wit, eyes that turned his

75

knees to pudding, and hair—oh, her glorious hair! A tongue like the lash of a whip, it was true, but he could break her of that, with kisses as searingly sweet as the one he'd stolen beneath the beech tree.

And she was, all but officially, already his. He would have to marry someday, especially if Charles didn't, and on that score Lesley was inclined to agree with his mother. At the memory of Amanda's slim body pressed beneath him, the delicate feel of her wrists trapped in his hands, he nearly turned the blacks toward Bond Street to thank his mother for threatening him into this betrothal.

At the moment Amanda despised him—or rather, despised what she *thought* he was—which meant at the earliest possible moment he must make a clean breast of things with her. He'd tell her tomorrow night, he decided, slowing the blacks before the park entrance. When he came to fetch her for Lady Cottingham's ball he'd be himself, in his best black evening dress, and sans the overdone Titus, which was beginning to itch beneath the band of his beaver hat.

But as the blacks made the turn into Hyde Park and Lesley drew them in to avoid running up the back of a phaeton with yellow wheels, the dapper figure of a slight man, dressed in gray and twirling a walking stick, caught his attention. With an all but imperceptable nod in Lesley's direction, he touched the tip of his cane to the brim of his hat and melted away into the throng of people hurrying along the flagway.

It was Fisk! Damn and blast the man, he was following him!

In his elation, Lesley had forgotten about the pesky little Runner, but remembering him and his promise that the gentleman in the black mask would appear again at Lady Cottingham's ball, cast his intention of revealing himself to Amanda in a new light. She knew about the thieves, just how, he wasn't sure, but she'd referred to them by name. The one called Smythe had struck Andrew (and he was immensely pleased to realize she really *had* been with her brother in his mother's garden), which raised a dozen burning questions Lesley longed to but didn't dare ask, for fear of involving her further in what might well prove to be—despite Fisk's assurances to the contrary—a nasty affair before it was finished.

Until his business with Fisk was concluded he must, to protect Amanda, maintain his charade and his silence. And the madly itching Titus, which was making his scalp prickle abominably. Relieving the worst of it with a quick scratch of the whip handle, Lesley turned on his pillow to face Amanda. The look on her face seemed pensive now rather than fretful.

"Would you do me the honor of accompanying me to Lady Cottingham's ball tomorrow evening?"

Thinking she'd rather throw herself under the wheels of his curricle, Amanda nonetheless forced herself to smile as she shifted on the seat to face Lord Earnshaw.

"I would be pleased, but are you sure you're up to it?"

"Up to it? What do you mean?"

"You can't dance with a cane, my lord."

"I've no intention of dancing with a cane," Lesley replied, clenching his teeth to keep from shouting. "I intend to dance with *you*."

"But, my lord—" Amanda began, then glanced at the cushion beneath him. "Is your injury the reason for the pillow? Why ever didn't you say so?"

There was no hint of blush or maidenly demure

in her question. Still, Lesley colored, from mounting frustration and temper, he told himself, not her unabashed gaze.

"No, that's *not* the reason for the pillow. Your concern is touching, but unnecessary, I assure you. I'm not so feeble I can't manage a set or two with my betrothed."

My betrothed, Amanda repeated silently, the sudden, sinking panic she felt striking her with fresh inspiration.

"You needn't put on a brave face with me. That you've suffered such a grievous injury in the service of your country is proof enough of your courage. I shall accompany you to Lady Cottingham's, my lord, but I will *not* dance."

"Lesley," he ground out between still clenched teeth. "And the wound is not grievous, it is merely—"

"You are too brave to minimize it, but my mind is quite made up. We shall find comfortable chairs to sit in and drink punch." Amanda gave him a brilliant, sunburst smile. "I shall even carry your pillow for you! As proudly and humbly as you bear your wound!"

Outflanked and outwitted again, Lesley realized, wondering if his mother would miss Teddy if he murdered him.

"Very well," he gave in with a sigh. "I shall call for you at half-past nine."

Amanda nodded, a serene and suspiciously smug smile on her face. He'd told his mother he would escort her and so he would, but if her expression was any indication, Lesley doubted she'd miss him when he made an early end to the evening to do Fisk's bidding.

It was a singularly bleak and deflating thought.

Chapter Nine

At just past noon the next day a second horrendous
shriek rocked the Gilbertson household, catching
Andrew in dishabille in the morning room with a
cup of coffee quavering precariously toward his
mouth. His already throbbing temples pulsed sickeningly, but since his nerves were steadier than
Lord Hampton's (he was only Amanda's brother,
not her father), he splashed just his hand and the
tablecloth as he returned the cup to its saucer.

Hissing between his teeth, he winced and sucked
his burnt fingers into his mouth as his twin burst
into the room with a crumpled copy of the morning
Times clenched in one hand and the furies of Hell
blazing in her eyes.

"*Where* is Papa?" she shouted.

"Mandy, *please*," Andrew begged hoarsely, abandoning his fingers to cradle his head. "Have a care
for a dying man."

"Where *is* he?" she shrieked again and stamped
her foot.

"Out—" Andrew gasped, and downed his coffee
in one fiery gulp. It scalded all the way to his stom-

ach, but he held his breath until the flames and the urge to cast up his accounts died, then fixed a baleful, bleary gaze on Amanda. "Took Mama for a drive. Said she looked pale."

"Oh, how cowardly! *He* is the pale one!" Amanda stormed to the sideboard and began slamming the lids on the breakfast chafing dishes. "How *dare* he! Oh, how *could* he! I will *never* forgive him! Never, ever, *ever!*"

She kept raging and banging; the silver lids crashing and ringing in Andrew's head. His stomach rolled ominously, and the walls began to wobble. Snatching up the china coffee server, he drained the contents and collapsed, head in his arms on the tabletop, until Amanda's tantrum had run its course. He raised his head, then, found the room had steadied itself, and an expression of distaste on his sister's face.

"Really, Andy. Someone else might have wanted coffee."

"Leave off," he growled, "and kindly come down from the boughs long enough to tell me why Papa is a coward."

"Read this." Amanda threw the wadded *Times* at him.

The crackle of the paper as he smoothed it made Andrew's teeth grate, but he steeled himself against it, blinked and squinted, and at last brought the print into focus sufficient to read the announcement of Amanda's engagement to Captain Lord Lesley Earnshaw.

"Let me be the first to express my felicitations," he said.

"Do so," Amanda warned, her eyes flashing again, "and it will be the *last* thing you ever express to anyone!"

"But you were told the match would be arranged, to consider yourself betrothed. I was sitting beside you when Papa said it."

"And where were you yesterday when that—that—*creature* he intends to marry me to called?" Amanda gave him a challenging glare and thrust her fists on her hips. "You went haring off with your dissolute friends when you should've been *here* to support me!"

"Support you!" Andrew shouted, regretting it as his temples thudded anew. "You mean take your side against Papa, which you know I *cannot* do!"

"You mean you *won't*!"

"I *can't*!"

"You would if you'd *seen* him!"

"Mandy, *really*," Andrew *tsked*. "Overdoing it a bit, aren't you, calling Captain Earnshaw a creature?"

"Am I? Be at Lady Cottingham's this evening and see for yourself." She flounced toward the door, but whirled back and flung at him haughtily, "That is, if you can spare the time from your precious friends!"

This was too much. Andrew leaped up from the table and charged down the hallway behind her, holding his temples, and with his banyan flapping around him like a sail.

"Now see here—" he began, just as they reached the foyer, and Lord and Lady Hampton came through the door.

A gust of breeze, warm with the smoky fragrance of dying leaves, entered with them. They were smiling, their cheeks pinked, but at the expression on their daughter's face, their eyes widened, and Lady Hampton went pale.

"How dare you!" Amanda accused, breathless

81

with fury. "How *dare* you send an announcement of my engagement without my permission, let alone my acceptance!"

"Careful, Mandy," Andrew warned, sidling up behind her to rest a hand on her shoulder.

"How dare you use that tone with me," Lord Hampton retorted icily.

"I beg pardon, but I—" Amanda's voice broke, and Andrew felt a sob shudder through her. "Oh, Papa, how could you *do* this to me?"

"Amanda, you're crying!" Lady Hampton shrilled, wavering between clinging to her husband's arm and rushing to her daughter. "Bennett, what on earth have you done?"

Lord Hampton's brows leapt up his forehead. "I've done nothing!"

"Oh, Mama!" Amanda flung herself into her mother's arms. "He's the most *awful* man! A popinjay! A fop, a—a—*creature*!"

"There, darling," Lady Hampton soothed and stroked her hair. "You're overset, I know, but you shouldn't speak so of your father."

"Not *me*, Cornelia!" Lord Hampton roared. "She means Earnshaw!"

"Do *not* shout at me!" Lady Hampton returned imperiously. "I'll speak to *you* later, my lord!"

Cradling her daughter in her arms, she led her away up the stairs. Amanda dropped a surreptitious wink to Andrew over the bannister, then laid her cheek on her mother's shoulder and sniffled.

So that's the game, he thought, divide and conquer. He recalled the tactic from Julius Caesar, and decided Latin was another thing Amanda should never have been taught.

"I need a brandy," Lord Hampton said feelingly,

shoving his hat and driving gloves at a footman, and beating a harried retreat to his study.

Andrew joined him, in the brandy as well as the study. His first swallow took his breath away, but his second, at last, eased the throb in his temples.

"Surely Mandy exaggerates about Lord Earnshaw," he said.

"Of course she does," Lord Hampton returned swiftly.

Perhaps a bit too swiftly, thought Andrew, noting the sudden flush which rose past his shirt points.

"I thought we were out of this damned coil," Lord Hampton grumbled, throwing himself in his chair.

"Coil?" Andrew echoed. "How is this a coil, sir? The match is made. There's naught to do but post the banns and arrange the wedding."

"Perhaps if you spoke to Amanda," his father suggested, straightening hopefully in his chair. "You can explain things to her better than I."

"What things?" Andrew asked calmly, trying to shield his sudden unease.

"Assure her Lord Earnshaw's—er—current mode of dress is but temporary. A passing thing, if you will. He said as much to me in private yesterday."

There was a definite note of eagerness—or was it desperation?—in his father's voice. Just who is he trying to convince, Andrew wondered, Amanda or himself?

"I'll speak to her, sir," he promised, and went straight upstairs to confront his sister for particulars.

But Marie would not admit him. Lady Amanda, she claimed through a crack in the barely opened door of her mistress's bedchamber, had taken to her bed with a megrim.

"That's a bag of moonshine," Andrew retorted. "And if she thinks feigning illness will keep her from Lady Cottingham's, she'd best have another think."

"Oh, she'll be right as a trivet by this evenin'," Marie assured him cheerfully and shut the door in his face.

Andrew knew as well as the Duchess of Braxton that Amanda had never had a megrim in her life, which meant that what she'd taken to was hatching another scheme. A scheme that did not include him, which boded ill.

Perhaps his mother could shed some light. Andrew went along to her chamber, was told by her abigail that her ladyship was with his lordship, and then made his way downstairs. He could hear their voices from the hallway but couldn't make out what they were saying, not even when he unabashedly pressed his ear to the study door.

Feeling frustrated and ill used, Andrew gave himself over to his valet, then struck out for Jackson's to make his own inquiries. Between bouts he gleaned very little, for Captain Lord Earnshaw was best known among his set (due to his lengthy absence in the wars) as the Duke of Braxton's brother. There were only two brief reports of having seen him the day before with Amanda in Hyde Park, but beyond the height of his shirt points, which were considered well within the bounds of any Exquisite, there was nothing out of the ordinary.

Next Andrew tried Boodles, where he was given the direction of Sir Alex Hawksley, a known intimate of Lord Earnshaw. But at that gentleman's rooms he was told Sir Alex was recovering from a shaving accident and was not receiving callers.

On the whole, it was a long and exasperating day.

In a sour mood and late for Lady Cottingham's, Andrew made his way home to find Amanda had already left with Lord Earnshaw, and his parents for an evening of whist with the Duchess of Braxton.

Card party my foot, he thought, the unease that had plagued him all day hurrying him through his toilette sans the assistance of his fusspot valet. At half-past ten he arrived at Lady Cottingham's brilliantly lit Grosnevor Square mansion, impeccably, if hastily, turned out.

It was an absolute crush, the saloons packed to the cornices with the beau monde. A social coup for Lady Cottingham, a statuesque matron preening in the midst of the throng in turquoise silk, but a nightmare for Andrew trying to squirm his way through it to the ballroom.

The evening had retained the warmth of the afternoon, and though every door and window was open, it was still near stifling. When he came upon a tray of champagne borne by a footman, Andrew helped himself to a glassful. He knocked it back thirstily, unmindful of the startled flicker that crossed the footman's face as he turned quickly away and disappeared into the crowd.

"It don't fadge, I tell you," came a low male voice from an alcove behind and to the right of Andrew. "The Lesley Earnshaw I knew at Oxford wouldn't be caught dead with a quizzing glass. There's something demmed strange about him, and no mistaking that."

Startled by the innuendo, Andrew cocked his head to one side to listen.

"Mayhap it's the French musket ball he stopped. I heard it took him in the knee, but Paget says it caught him—er—" the respondent paused to chuckle lewdly "—in a more delicate location."

Innuendo be damned, this was grounds for naming seconds! Spinning on one heel to confront the gossipers, Andrew nearly collided with a deb in green taffeta and her escort, begged their pardon, and stepped back. The couple acknowledged his apology with a nod and moved away to reveal the alcove, empty now except for a potted fig.

Andrew could do nothing but frown, mutter an oath, and strike off again for the ballroom, where the crush was worse near the high, wide archway leading onto the marble dance floor. Over the turbaned heads of two stout dowagers, he saw it was jammed with couples, as were the chairs lining the walls. Craning his neck, Andrew bobbed and ducked the headdresses in front of him in search of Amanda.

"Mind you, we have only Matilda Blumfield's word she actually *kissed* the rogue," said the matron on his left, "but it wouldn't surprise me. She's bear-led Cornelia for years! It's her just desserts, I say!"

"Poor Hampton had no choice but to try to save face with that hasty engagement," replied her companion. "Still, I feel sorry for the gel, and I do *not* agree with Matilda that half a man is better than none."

Behind them, Andrew was frozen in mid-bob between fury and apoplexy. Half a man! Just desserts! If his father didn't throttle old Blumfield for breaking her vow of silence he swore he'd do it himself.

And then he'd throttle his father, he decided, at last understanding what it was he wanted him to explain to Amanda. But first things first. His most urgent priority was to find her and whisk her out of here before she heard the latest on dit.

With a brisk and sudden snap, the two dowagers opened their fans and moved out of the archway. Andrew cast a sour frown after them as he stepped into the ballroom, and someone tugged his right sleeve.

"Where have you been?" Amanda hissed, pulling him around to face her.

"Where's Earnshaw?" Andrew caught her shoulders in his hands and scanned the room over the top of her head.

"Never mind *him*. Our friend Smythe is here."

"How do you know?" Andrew demanded, his grip on her tightening. "You didn't get a good look at him. Or *did* you?"

"Andy, that hurts!" Amanda slapped his hands away and frowned. "And of course I didn't get a good look at him, but it's him just the same!"

"What makes you think so?"

"Because he's rigged out like a footman, just as he was at the Duchess of Braxton's, and when he served me punch a while ago his eyes nearly popped out of his head. I've been looking for him ever since."

"Has anyone said anything to you?"

"No-o-o, but I've been getting the oddest looks." Her brow furrowing perplexedly, Amanda turned her back to him and peered over her left shoulder. "Does my petticoat show?"

"No," Andrew replied, grateful that no one had given her the cut direct. "Where's Earnshaw?"

"In the chair I left him in, I'm sure." One corner of her mouth quirked distastefully. "I am *not* going to marry him, Andy. I'm telling you what I intend to tell Papa in the morning. He can beat me, starve me, disown me, I don't care. I will *not* marry Lesley Earnshaw."

"You're damned right you won't." He took her arm, drew her further into the room and stopped. "Where is he?"

"Oh, Andy, you're the most wonderful brother!" Amanda cried joyously and hugged him fiercely.

"Of course I am," he agreed, unwrapping her arms from his ribcage. "Now take me to Earnshaw."

"Whatever for?"

"Because the megrim you had this morning has come upon you again, and I'm going to take you home."

"And leave Smythe to rob Lady Cottingham blind? I think not!"

Indignantly, Amanda spun away from him, but Andrew pulled her back.

"Think on this. If you get yourself into another scrape, the Regent himself won't be able to dissuade Papa from marrying you off to Earnshaw."

"Hmmm, good point," she granted pensively. "I hadn't thought of that."

"Which means more to you?"

"Need you ask? Come along then, and I'll make my excuses."

Leaning on Andrew's arm and looking ill, Amanda steered him through the crowd toward the far side of the room. But when they reached the red cut velvet chair where she'd left Earnshaw, there was only his ebony stick leaning against it.

"How odd that he'd leave his cane." Amanda frowned puzzledly and picked it up. "He can't take a step without it."

"Obviously he can or he wouldn't have left it." Andrew took her arm and the lead. "Come on, we'll have to find him. And don't forget you have the headache."

Chapter Ten

And so did Lesley, as he combed Lady Cottingham's house in search of Amanda. The cause was only partly the sickeningly sweet punch he'd been sipping all evening; mostly it was fury at being abandoned and irritation at his stupidity, for it had taken him a good half hour to connect Amanda's sudden departure and lengthy absence from his side to the footman who'd served their last glass of punch.

Where in blazes *was* she? She'd been gone a devilishly long time, and worry was beginning to erode Lesley's ire as he paused in the card room doorway to scan the tables. The four matrons seated closest to him cast a startled look in his direction and then lowered their eyes, two of them giggling girlishly. At the table next to theirs, Lord Cottingham winked at his partner, a white-haired peer unknown to Lesley, who turned toward him, guffawed, and then buried his nose in his cards.

What the devil, he wondered, and glanced over his shoulder. Behind him loomed Sir Alex Hawksley, his left arm in a white linen sling.

"Hullo, Alex. So it's you they're sniggering at."

"No, I'm fairly certain it's you," Hawksley replied matter-of-factly. "Or perhaps it's your reticule. Clashes rather badly with your waistcoat."

Lesley glanced down and saw Amanda's beaded bag clenched in his right fist. She'd left it hanging on the back of her chair when she'd gone off to speak to Lady Cottingham (or so she'd said). He'd been fingering the beads—the same shade of sapphire as her eyes and her gown, which had turned his mouth dry at first sight of her in it—wondering what was keeping her when he'd realized the significance of the startled expression that crossed her face when the footman had served them. Obviously, he'd snatched it up as he'd leaped to his feet and come looking for her, although he didn't remember doing so.

"I'm trying to find the lady this belongs to," he told Hawksley. "Do you know Amanda Gilbertson? Have you by any chance seen her?"

"I've not had the pleasure." Sir Alex grinned and extended his hand. "Congratulations, Lesley. Quite a surprise, I must say. Hadn't a clue you were in the petticoat line."

"Neither did I," he admitted, distractedly surveying the crowded corridor outside the card room while Hawksley pumped his hand. "Where in deuces *is* she?"

"What's this?" Sir Alex laughed. "Left you at the gate already, has she? Clever chit."

Lesley had pivoted away from him for a better view of the hallway but wheeled back at the remark. He was smiling, but his hazel eyes flashed.

"Have a care, Alex. I'd hate to see you end with both arms in a sling."

Hawksley laughed again, a great, booming laugh

in keeping with his size, which drew Amanda's attention to him as she emerged on Andrew's arm from a saloon a short distance down the corridor. At first glance she didn't recognize the man facing him or the reticule he held. It wasn't until she'd started in the opposite direction that she realized the bag was hers—and the gentleman was Captain Lord Earnshaw.

The realization gave her such a jolt she almost pulled Andrew off his feet as she spun around, agape. Lesley's cane cut a circle in midair with her and whacked Andrew soundly behind the knee.

"Ouch! Damn it, Mandy, be careful with that thing!" He bent to rub his leg but straightened at the thunderstruck expression on his sister's face. "What is it? Is it Smythe?"

"No!" Amanda breathed. "It's Lord Earnshaw!"

"Where?"

"In the doorway with the man whose arm is in a sling."

Andrew spotted Hawksley instantly—it would have been difficult to miss a man of his size, even without the sling—but there was no awful fop—no popinjay. He craned his neck but saw only an elegantly turned out gentleman holding a beaded blue reticule.

"I don't see him."

"How can you not? He's holding my reticule!"

Andrew looked again, intently this time. The man's shirt points were a bit on the high side, his brocade waistcoat somewhat vivid for evening, but other than that . . .

"Mandy," he said firmly, giving her a hard look. "If that's Lord Earnshaw, then one of us desperately needs spectacles. Of all the words I might use to describe that particular gentleman, creature is *not* one of them."

"I know, but I tell you, it's *him*," Amanda insisted.

But how did I overlook him, she marveled, watching Earnshaw clap his companion on his good shoulder and turn toward her. The movement brought him closer to a brace of candles, which gleamed his dark hair with blue highlights as he craned his neck in her direction. His jaw was set and his eyes flashed as brilliantly as the diamond stick pin in his cravat. Amanda felt herself shiver, and she realized suddenly that she hadn't the faintest idea what color his eyes were.

"He's looking for someone," she said to Andrew.

"Dunce," he replied shortly, and pulled her forward. "He's looking for you."

And obviously he'd seen her. The twitch of a muscle in Lord Earnshaw's clenched jaw and the narrowing of his eyelids told Amanda so, but she had just a momentary glimpse of his slitted gaze before Andrew drew her into the crowd and her view of him was obscured. When they emerged from the throng seconds later, the large man with his arm in a sling had disappeared, and Lord Earnshaw was leaning against the doorframe.

His demeanor had changed so completely and so swiftly that Amanda came to an abrupt, open-mouthed halt in front of him. The broad shoulders he'd squared as he'd turned toward her were slumped, his clenched jaw lax. Moments before he'd stood firmly on both feet, but now his left knee was bent, and he held his foot gingerly off the floor.

This was not the man she'd glimpsed through the crowd. This was the fop who sat on a pillow, the cavalry officer who crossed the leads. But which one, Amanda wondered, her suspicions aroused, was the real Captain Earnshaw?

"There you are, Amanda." Lesley straightened from the slouch he'd fallen into when he'd seen her with his cane and realized that he had, in his anger and consternation, left the damned thing leaning against his chair. Raising his quizzing glass, he peered down his nose at Andrew. "And who is this?"

"My brother, Viscount Welsey," she replied. "Andrew, may I present Captain Lord Lesley Earnshaw."

"Ah, my soon-to-be brother-in-law," Lesley said and limply offered his hand.

The same day cows fly, thought Andrew. "My congratulations," he said, making quick work of the handshake.

"Bless you," Lesley said to Amanda. "You've brought my cane."

"And you've fetched my reticule," she replied. "How thoughtful."

The exchange of possessions was made, Lesley indulging the urge he'd felt all evening to touch her by deliberately tangling his fingers with hers. Much to his surprise, she colored very prettily and did not shrink from his touch.

"Not fetched, my dear, recovered," he corrected, "from the footman who lifted it from the back of your chair."

"Footman!" Amanda shot Andrew a wide-eyed look. "Did you catch him?"

"I did *try*," Lesley replied petulantly, "but I lost him in the crowd. He knew I was on to him, though, for I found your reticule on the floor. He dropped it, I'm sure, rather than risk being caught with it."

"Did you tell Lord Cottingham?" Andrew asked hopefully.

"Tell him what? I didn't actually *see* the man take it, I merely noticed it missing a moment or so after he'd passed by, put two and two together, and gave chase." Lesley ended the lie with a sniff and rubbed his leg. "Best as I could, of course."

"You went after him without your cane?"

"I didn't think of it." Lesley shrugged indifferently, aware that Amanda was staring at him sharply and rather calculatingly. "I'm unused to infirmity."

"Would you recognize him if you saw him again?" she asked.

"Possibly." Lesley pursed his lips thoughtfully. "I couldn't be sure unless I did, of course, but he could very well be the footman who last served us punch."

Amanda shot Andrew a triumphant smile, which was all the confirmation Lesley needed to be sure that she had, indeed, recognized the thief. And it was, he decided abruptly, time for the man in the black mask to appear.

"We must tell Lord Cottingham at once," Amanda said eagerly. "He can call the staff together, and—"

"In the midst of *this*?" Lesley interrupted, waving one hand at the guests chatting and laughing as they traversed the corridor.

"But the man is a thief!" Amanda declared vehemently.

A little too vehemently, thought Lesley. And so did Andrew, who frowned at his sister's overbright eyes.

"An *attempted* thief," he pointed out.

"Exactly so," Lesley agreed. "Had I caught him

with your reticule, then certainly charges could've been brought. Because I did not, there's nothing his lordship can do."

"Nothing *he* can do, perhaps, but *I* do not intend—"

"*A-man-da.*" Andrew made three terse syllables of her name and took a firm grasp on her elbow. "Do you recall the matter we thought to discuss with Papa in the morning?"

The reminder put a thorough period to whatever it was she'd been about to say. The charming flush drained from her cheeks and the sparkle went out of her eyes. Regretfully, perhaps even guiltily, Lesley thought, she glanced at him, then lowered her gaze.

"I suppose you're right," she acquiesced, but most unconvincingly.

"Of course we are," said Andrew.

The relief in his voice passed as a fair imitation of condescension, which earned him an indignant glare from Amanda. There's something afoot here, thought Lesley, regretting that he couldn't stay to ferret it out.

"The thrill of the chase has badly overtaxed me," he said, mopping his brow with a lace handkerchief withdrawn from his waistcoat. "I fear I must beg your leave, Amanda, and trust your brother to see you safely home."

"Let us accompany you," Andrew responded quickly, seizing the chance to remove Amanda from harm's way.

"I won't hear of it. I insist you stay and enjoy yourselves."

"Oh, but—"

"Let's please stay," Amanda interrupted, casting

Andrew a meaningful glance. "I haven't danced all evening."

"There you are, Welsey," said Lesley, leaning on his cane to bow to Amanda. "How can you refuse?"

The dubious, distrustful gleam in her eyes as she offered her hand and he raised it to kiss touched a finger of unease to the nape of Lesley's neck. If he hadn't known better, he would've sworn he'd somehow given himself away.

"Perhaps," he murmured, raising just his eyes to her face, "I should have danced with my cane after all."

"Perhaps you should have," Amanda agreed, shivering at the warm brush of his breath on her fingertips.

"You may have my waltz, Welsey." He made Andrew a small bow and gently squeezed Amanda's hand. "Good evening."

Smiling, he loosed her fingers and turned away. Were his eyes blue, Amanda wondered, or were they green? Dazed and somewhat breathless, she watched him make his halting way through the crowd, until she noticed the irregularity of his step and her brows drew together speculatively.

"Andy," she asked slowly, "which leg is Lord Earnshaw favoring?"

"Why—" Andrew paused to study his retreating figure "—his right, I believe."

"I'd swear to you that yesterday he favored his left."

"What? But that would mean—" His eyelids took a leap and he wheeled toward Amanda. "Are you sure?"

"I'm certain."

"How *dare* he!" A fierce glint sprang into Andrew's eyes and he started after Lesley.

"Don't be a fool." Amanda caught his sleeve. "Do you forget Lord Earnshaw has fought two duels?"

"That—that *creature*"—Andrew spluttered furiously—"couldn't fight his way out of a badly tied cravat!"

"Yes," Amanda agreed pensively, "or so it would appear. Why didn't I tumble to that straight off?"

"Now that you mention it, why didn't I?" Andrew frowned unhappily. "I should have this morning, when you were going on about how niminy-piminy he is. But what I can't fathom is why he's gone to such lengths."

"Can't you? It's obvious!" Amanda snapped waspishly. "He no more wants to marry me than I want to marry him! He's trying to make me cry off!"

"And you most definitely *will*," Andrew responded forcefully. "And once we make things clear to him, with Papa's complete support, I'm sure."

"That's some consolation, I suppose," Amanda muttered ruefully.

"Then why are you looking so Friday-faced? I'd have thought you'd be turning handsprings."

"I'm not! I mean, I am—I mean—"

Aware that she was stammering, and feeling inexplicably flustered, Amanda stopped herself and raised one hand to her cheeks. Odd. She didn't feel Friday-faced. She felt—flushed. Yet her fingertips were icy, and none too steady.

Andrew was staring at her as if she'd just grown another head and, as bewildered as she felt, for all she knew she had. Maybe that was why Lord Earnshaw didn't want to marry her.

"I'll be fine once I've had time to digest all this and Papa has released me from this travesty of an engagement."

Her reply sounded as hollow to her as it obviously did to Andrew. He raised a questioning brow, but otherwise did not remark upon it as he took her arm and led her through Lady Cottingham's house to the foyer. When he suggested she fetch her wrap, Amanda was still so befuddled she merely nodded and started up the sweeping staircase while he went to summon the carriage.

Most of her daze had worn off, however, by the time she'd reached the lavish bedchamber set aside for the use of the ladies and the abigail there had helped her locate the cape that matched her gown. Sitting down with it in a corner where the candlelight didn't quite reach, she considered her reaction to the discovery of Lord Earnshaw's treachery.

It was one thing to scheme and connive, but quite another, as she had just so painfully learned, to find oneself the object of such duplicity. She'd taken the blow in her pride rather than her heart (or so she told herself), but it was no less hurtful. Perhaps even more so when it struck her that she hadn't been rejected by the limp-wristed fop who'd taken her driving, but by the dashing man with blue-black hair whom she'd had a glimpse of in the corridor.

The realization left her feeling ugly, undesirable, and tearful. Hastily, Amanda rose and flung her cape around her shoulders, then started as two ladies of her mother's set, the Countess Featherston and Lady Ingram, swept into the room. Averting her face, she retreated into the shadows to regain her composure before making her presence known.

The countess sat down at the dressing table to experiment among the collection of fragrances arranged in crystal vials while Lady Ingram tipped a tall cheval glass in its frame to better examine the hem of her gown.

"Believe as you will," she said, turning from side to side, "but I refuse to credit anything Matilda Blumfield says, or to give Cornelia's daughter the cut direct on the basis of such a preposterous tale." She paused to sniff and tug at her waist sash. "Indirect, perhaps, but only if she actually kissed the thief."

The comment struck Amanda like a blow. Horror, fury, and shame washed over her in the same wave. Her eyes widened, her mouth went slack, and she shrank deeper into the shadows as the countess turned on the bench to face her companion.

"But don't you find her hasty engagement to what's left of Eugenia's son sufficient proof?" She rejoined archly. "You should, because you know as well as I that the gel's been on the road to rack and ruin since her come out."

" 'Tis a pity about Lesley, though," Lady Ingram sighed wistfully. "He did so put me in mind of his father." She sniffed again, her nose wrinkling distastefully. "*Before* he went to war, that is."

Strangely, it was the slur on Lord Earnshaw that jolted Amanda out of her shocked stupor. Her chin lifted defiantly and her fingers curled into fists of rage, but she waited until the two ladies had finished the repair to their toilettes and left before stepping into the light.

Now she understood the strange looks she'd been receiving all evening. No one had given her the cut yet, and no one would until the *ton* had had time to thoroughly discuss her transgression and decide on appropriate censure. At best, Amanda gauged she had twenty-four hours to mount a counteroffensive to Matilda Blumfield's slander.

Only four days ago she'd been willing to risk the baroness's tongue and social ruin to escape Lesley Earnshaw, but now that it stared her in the face, she was, beneath her fury, more frightened than she'd ever been in her life. Even more than she had been up the beech tree in the Duchess of Braxton's garden with Smythe and Jack and Harry peering at her and Andrew.

And ironically, she had no one to blame but herself. She'd told the lie about kissing the gentleman in the black mask—only it was the truth, which was even worse. Why oh why, Amanda groaned, hadn't she swooned and fallen unconscious beside her mother?

It was a temptation to do so now, but that would do nothing to get her out of this coil, and she had to extricate herself—*somehow*—but at the moment she hadn't a clue how. Fastening her cape and looping her reticule over her wrist, Amanda made for the door, praying fervently that genius would strike her with a brilliant plan.

It did, even sooner than she'd dared hope, as she stopped halfway down the staircase to search the crowded foyer for Andrew. As she leaned partway over the polished ebony banister for a better view, her attention was drawn to a near collision beneath her between a stout middle-aged lord and a footman bearing an empty tray.

The servant's bow and hasty back step was acknowledged with an imperious nod, and the gentleman continued on his way, oblivious to the loss of the thumbnail-sized ruby which had moments before nestled in the folds of his cravat. The jewel winked briefly in the palm of the footman's hand, then disappeared into the pocket of his livery jacket as he shouldered his tray and made unhurriedly for a narrow servant's passage beneath the stairs.

It was Smythe, Amanda realized, on a sharp gasp of revelation. Her salvation and her redemption!

Chapter Eleven

By the time supper was announced, Andrew still had not found Amanda. From long years of experience he'd realized much quicker than Lesley that he'd been abandoned, but that made his sister's disappearance no less worrisome. In fact it made it more so, for he'd guessed what she was about.

It came to him in a flash of memory when the music stopped and the guests in twos and fours began drifting toward the supper room. He remembered then, crouching on a limb of the beech tree and whispering to Amanda that if he were the thief he'd strike while the guests were at table.

With a groan of dread, Andrew surmised Amanda must also have remembered, and considering her engagement to Lord Earnshaw all but dissolved, had gone to ground to await Smythe's move. Unfortunately, knowing why was no help in determining where, which left him no choice but to find himself a bolt hole and wait for events to unfold.

Cursing himself for trusting her uncharacteristic docility, Andrew made his way cautiously through Lady Cottingham's house, silent now, but for the echo of chatter from the guests at supper in the wing adjacent. Much as he loved his sister, Andrew was out of patience with her (this was, after all, her second disappearance in twice as many days), very nearly out of sympathy, and not at all sure he could save her from their father's wrath if this ended in another fiasco.

On tiptoe he reached the foyer, unaware of the Baroness Blumfield creeping along behind him. As Andrew ducked around one of the thick marble pillars supporting the domed ceiling, the baroness, her beady eyes agleam, nipped behind the polished suit of armor standing guard at the foot of the stairs.

Neither she or Andrew had long to wait. Within moments Smythe appeared, clutching a bulging sack to his chest. Glancing warily from side to side, he passed within inches of the pillar. Andrew slid quickly out from behind it in his wake, but too late to get a good look at his face.

He had just a glimpse of a lantern jaw and long nose before Smythe disappeared into the corridor that led to the ballroom and four other saloons, all of which connected and opened onto the terrace and the garden through French doors. Andrew followed as close as he dared, still unmindful of the baroness dogging his heels.

At the end of the corridor he inched around the corner to reconnoiter and saw Amanda, wearing her cape and tucking her slippers into her reticule, creep silently into the ballroom. Andrew ran after her, the soles of his pumps sliding on the polished floor and almost upending him as he cut too sharply through the archway.

At the clatter of his footsteps behind her, Amanda spun around and started visibly. So did Smythe, who paused only long enough to fling his sack over his shoulder before springing like a hare for the French doors.

"Stop, thief!" Andrew shouted, he hoped loud enough to draw servants.

"Now look what you've done!" Amanda cried, breaking into a run. "He's getting away!"

"Mandy, stop!" He shouted, but she only ran faster, which left him no choice but to give chase.

Shoeless, she was fleet as a deer as she raced through the French doors no more than a half-dozen paces behind Smythe. In his treacherous pumps, Andrew did well to lose no ground on her as he slid out of the house and to a halt on the flagstone terrace.

By the glow of the lanterns strung to light the garden, he saw Smythe deftly vault the low terrace wall, and Amanda, who'd gained perhaps two steps on him, let go of her skirts to scramble over behind him. The hem of her gown tore with an audible rip as she did, leaving a silken scrap for Andrew to pluck free of the stones as he followed her.

If he hadn't tripped on something as he launched himself over the wall and subsequently came down wrong on a rough tuft of grass when he landed, he might have caught her. His foot twisted viciously, and though he tried to keep running, his throbbing ankle simply would not permit it.

"Damnit, Mandy, stop!" Andrew shouted, limping, wincing, and falling farther behind.

On the flat sweep of lawn Smythe's lead on Amanda began to dwindle. He was taller and stronger, but his sack was obviously heavy and beginning to slow him down. Once they'd cleared the shadow of the house and the oblong patches of light thrown by the windows, there was only a pale sliver of moon to wink dully on the braided trim of

Smythe's livery and gleam on Amanda's streaming hair.

Though feeble, the light was sufficient for Andrew to gauge she'd intercept Smythe before he reached the spiked wrought-iron fence enclosing Lord and Lady Cottingham's property. Fearing for her safety, Andrew hobbled after her as fast as his wrenched ankle allowed. He shouted at her and at Smythe, but his voice was drowned by the hellacious racket raised by the sack bouncing across Smythe's back, and that racket prevented Andrew from hearing the thunder of horse hooves behind him.

A second later Lucifer streaked past him, so close his streaming tail lashed his face. Crying out in alarm, Andrew flung up one arm to shield his eyes from the dirt and turf raining on him, then dragged his sleeve away and blinked in open-mouthed amazement at the horseman bearing down on Amanda.

Leaning to the right and all but falling off his mount, he scooped his arm around her and lifted her off her feet. Amanda shrieked, kicking and flailing as he struggled her onto the saddle in front of him. Lucifer went halfway up on his hindquarters beneath them, raked the darkness with his front hooves, and whinnied shrilly.

The piercing sound spun Smythe in his tracks. At the sight of the stallion rearing over him and the glint of moonlight on his shod hooves, his jaw went slack and the sack slipped off his shoulder. It hit the ground with a crash and he was off for the fence, his arms and legs pumping like mad.

The horseman pursued him for a yard or two, then abruptly wheeled the stallion to face Andrew. Lucifer danced and gnawed his bit, close enough for him to see the sheen of black silk tied around his rider's face.

Struck dumb, Andrew could only gape as Amanda twisted in the man's grasp, beheld his mask and froze with her hands clamped on the arm encircling her waist. The gentleman in the black mask gave Andrew a jaunty salute, then dug his heels in his stallion's flanks and sent him back the way he'd come.

"*A-n-d-y!*" Amanda screamed, as Lucifer thundered past, hailing him again with clods of turf, and bound for the near fence enclosing the lawn.

Realizing he meant to jump it, Andrew forgot his sprain as he wheeled after the stallion and made a lunge for Amanda. His ankle buckled and sent him sprawling on the grass. Winded and helpless, he could only watch as Lucifer, head up and ears pitched forward, bore down on the fence. When he launched himself at it, Andrew caught and held his breath.

And so did Amanda, her eyes closed, certain that she and her captor were about to be impaled on the spikes. But the stallion cleared them handily, with hardly a bump to announce their landing on the other side. He cantered several yards farther before the gentleman in the black mask reined him and turned him around.

Opening her eyes, Amanda saw they were in the garden of the adjacent property. The stallion, blowing and stamping his hooves, stood within a topiary hedge. It was too dark to make out the shapes, but there was enough light cast by the torches guttering above the heads of the footmen clustered on Lord and Lady Cottingham's lawn to show her Andrew, with Smythe's sack in his hand, being clapped on the back and assisted toward the house.

"Well, if that isn't the outside of enough!" she fumed indignantly, pushing her ruined hairdo out of her face. "They're crying Andy a hero!"

The deep chuckle in her ear reminded Amanda where she was, and of the dreams inspired by her brief encounter with this man in the Duchess of Braxton's garden. They'd been safe enough, she'd thought, for she never imagined she'd see him again. But now, feeling the strength in his arm circling her waist and the warmth of his chest supporting her on the front of his flat saddle, the vividness of the dreams came back to her, fanning a wave of heat and acute awareness through her body.

"I demand you set me down this instant," she said imperiously, not trusting herself to look at him.

"I beg my lady's pardon," he replied, the chuckle in his voice stirring a delicious shiver and the curls at the nape of her neck, "but you are hardly in a position to demand anything."

"A gentleman would not point that out."

"And a lady would not pursue a thief in the dark. Not without a very good reason."

"My reason is private. And exclusively my concern."

"Did *you*, perhaps, wish to be proclaimed a hero?"

"If you must know, yes," she snapped at him over her shoulder. "But thanks to you, I've failed."

"At least you are unharmed."

"Unharmed!" Amanda shrilled at him. "You cloth head! Don't you realize what you've done?"

"I believe," Lesley replied mildly, "that I may have saved your life."

"No! You—you idiot!" Amanda sputtered furiously. "You've compromised me! Which a gentleman would have realized *before* he swooped me up!"

"I hardly think your virtue is more important than your life."

"I'll have no life after this, you fool! Not unless *you* wish to marry me!"

"My lady," Lesley grinned wickedly, thoroughly enjoying himself and her fit of temper, "this is so sudden."

"But for *you* I'd have caught Smythe! I could have made him say he hadn't kissed me—"

"Did he?" Lesley cut in, clasping her shoulder in his free hand and turning her to face him.

"Of course not, you clunch, *you* did!" Amanda roughly pushed his hand away. "But Smythe would have said he didn't—because he *didn't*—and then I wouldn't be ruined!"

"What has Smythe to do with ruining you? You just said I ruined you."

"No, I said you compromised me. Smythe didn't ruin me—I ruined myself!"

"My lady," Lesley said slowly, striving for patience, "that's impossible. It doesn't come anywhere near sense."

"Oh, of course it does! It's as simple as you are!"

And in her outrage, Amanda proceeded to tell him the whole tale. She told him everything, the Baroness Blumfield overhearing her confession, Lord Hampton decreeing that she would marry Captain Lord Earnshaw—*everything*—in a furious outpouring.

Listening to her tell of the baroness falling through the saloon door, and of blacking her teeth, Lesley wanted to laugh. But by the time her narrative reached Lady Cottingham's ball, his giving himself away by limping on the wrong foot, and the conversation she'd overheard between Lady Ingram and the Countess Featherston, he wanted to climb down from Lucifer's back, yank his tail, and receive the swift kick in the war wound he so richly deserved.

"So you can see it's imperative I apprehend Smythe, can't you? He's my only hope of redemption." Amanda shifted on the front of the saddle to eye him appraisingly. "It occurs to me, since you and he are in the same line of work—and you'll want to do whatever you can to restore my reputation, since you helped destroy it—that you could be of assistance. Perhaps you and Smythe frequent the same establishments, have acquaintances in common—"

"I repeat, my lady," Lesley interrupted, "I know no one named Smythe. Or Jack. Or Harry."

"I didn't say you did, sir. I merely said—"

"I heard what you said," Lesley cut her off, the calculating gleam in her eyes reminding him of Mr. Fisk. "And I am telling you I am *not* a thief. I am, as you are, merely a victim of circumstance."

"Indeed? And what circumstance is it that requires a mask?"

"One I am not at liberty to divulge."

"How convenient. And how interesting that both times we've met you've been in Smythe's proximity—if not his company."

"And that proves I'm a thief?"

"It hardly disproves it."

"Then pray tell me, my lady, what have I stolen?"

My heart, Amanda realized, with a clarity that stunned her. Dark as it was, she could just see the outline of his face, his square jaw, the firm jut of his chin, and the tumble of his windswept hair above his mask. As it had in her dreams, her attention fixed on his mouth, the shape of it, the fullness of his lower lip, and she could almost feel him kissing her again.

It shook her so that she turned hastily away and saw Andrew, facing their direction on the Cottingham terrace with a torch raised above his head. He couldn't possibly see them, it was far too dark and they were too far away, yet Amanda shrank as he made a slow sweep with the torch and the flame guttered and sparked.

"Quickly! You must set me down and go! It's Andy—my brother—he's looking for me!"

"I cannot do that, my lady."

"Don't be a fool!" She cried over her shoulder. "Why not?"

"Because I do not wish to."

For the first time in her life, Amanda genuinely thought she might swoon. The words were by far the six most beautiful anyone had ever spoken to her, and like a healing balm closed the wound Captain Lord Earnshaw had inflicted on her pride.

"What *do* you wish to do?"

Kiss you, Lesley wanted to say, but instead replied, "Only see you safely home, if you'll give me your direction. Having compromised you, it seems the least I can do."

Amanda couldn't see the smile on his face, but she heard it in his voice. And she heard something else she couldn't identify. It wasn't familiarity, for beyond the few moments they'd spent beneath the beech tree, this man was a stranger to her. It was liken to intimacy, which was impossible, yet it was there, almost palpable between them. Because she couldn't put a name to it, Amanda knew it should frighten her, but it didn't. Nor did the man who held her in his arms.

Briefly, she glanced at Andrew, who was still

peering into the darkness. He must be frantic with worry, but apparently only he had witnessed her being taken up. He wouldn't give her away and would do his best to give a plausible account of her absence, yet she wasn't at all sure she could trust him not to cry an alarm if she called out to assure him of her safety.

"My father's house is in Hanover Square," Amanda replied, deciding that if she was to be ruined, she would have at least one pleasant memory to sustain her in spinsterhood.

"We are as good as there," Lesley replied, wheeling Lucifer at a canter across the lawn beyond the hedge.

There was a fortuitously unlocked gate in the fence at the back of the property, which he was able to negotiate without dismounting. He then set Lucifer at a walk along a circuitous path of back streets and alleyways that would take them to Hanover Square. Eventually.

In the meantime he intended to enjoy Amanda's nearness, and to think of a way to turn her up sweet, else this might well be his only chance to hold her in his arms. If it were merely a question of Mr. Fisk, he'd rip off his mask and Bow Street be damned. But Amanda already despised him for his duplicity, and he shuddered to think of her reaction to discovering Captain Lord Lesley Earnshaw had deceived her again.

"You are not seriously considering another attempt to capture Smythe, are you, my lady?"

"I *must*," she answered resolutely. "It's my only hope."

"But if marriage will save your reputation, and you are already betrothed—"

"To the most odious man in England," she put in

acidly. "And I wouldn't have Lesley Earnshaw now if he were the *last* odious man in England."

"Are you so certain your father will release you from your pledge?"

"If he doesn't, I'll—" Amanda faltered. She could hardly bear to think on it, but what if he did refuse? Her bag of tricks was nearly empty. "I'll think of something," she finished, managing to sound braver than she felt.

But she was trembling, and there was a slight tremor in her voice. Lesley hoped it was attributable to the nearness of his strong, manly self, but suspected it was more in anticipation of Lord Hampton's judgment. He was in a position to influence that decision, and he would, if it came to that, but he wanted Amanda to want him, to yearn for his touch, to love him as much as he loved her.

He wasn't sure when he'd fallen heels over ears for her. Perhaps when he'd discovered the bruise on his jaw, or when she'd looked at him so openly in his curricle and asked about his wound, mayhap not until tonight, when he'd realized she'd abandoned him, and it had struck him then that without her beside him his life—and his heart—would always be empty.

If he'd thought he could trust himself he would have held her closer, but the rub of her shoulder blades against his chest in rhythm with Lucifer's gait was driving him wild. Her hair smelled of lavender soap, and beneath his forearm, the span of her waist felt no larger than his wrist. He would have to go slowly with her, Lesley thought, and very tenderly on their wedding night.

Old cavalry horse that he was, Lucifer snorted and laid back his ears as he drew near the mouth of the narrow alleyway he'd been following under a loose rein. (It really was more to his credit than Lesley's that the damned Frenchie who'd shot him out of his stirrups had only made it painful to sit down for several weeks.) The voluntary stop he made alerted Lesley to the fact that they'd reached Hanover Square, and Amanda still thought he was the most odious man in England.

"That's the house." Amanda pointed. "The one with the capped brick wall and the oak tree overhanging it."

With the possible exception of the old beech in his mother's garden, trees as large as the oak soaring above the roof of Lord Hampton's house were uncommon in the city. It was a gargantuan thing, several of its larger limbs running parallel and broad as flagways to the balconies hung on the back of the house.

"See how the branches grow right up to the windows?" Amanda asked, pointing again. "I think it best if I go in that way."

"You mean up the tree? In a ball gown?"

"I've done it before, if you'll recall."

"As you wish, my lady."

Amanda, Lesley decided, as he goaded Lucifer into a walk, would definitely be the one to teach their children—two boys, he thought, and a girl with mahogany hair and sapphire eyes—the finer points of tree climbing.

The wall was high enough to hide Lucifer from any Nosey Parker servants who might be awake, and enough leaves still clung to the branches of the oak to screen Amanda as she climbed. It was a long, dizzying way up, thought Lesley, feeling a bit queasy as he eased Lucifer to a halt beside the wall and tipped back his head to look.

"You've climbed this gnarly old monster before, I trust?"

"Hundreds of times. Will your horse allow me to stand a moment on the saddle so I may reach the top of the wall?"

"Lucifer will allow a beautiful woman anything."

"Spanish coin, sir," Amanda rebuked, but smiled as she ducked her head to make sure her cape was fastened and her reticule securely looped over her wrist.

"I've been thinking, my lady. If you do end up being ruined, perhaps you could take up thievery."

Amanda raised just her eyes to his face. "That is a jest in very poor taste, sir."

"It's not a jest. I'm perfectly serious. You were born for the work."

"Is that a professional appraisal?"

"No. Merely the opinion of one of your victims."

"But I've taken nothing from you!"

"Oh, but you have, my lady," Lesley replied tenderly and cradled her cheek in his free hand. "You've taken my heart."

The graze of his fingertips raised gooseflesh and stirred a shiver at the base of her spine. Savoring the caress, Amanda closed her eyes and leaned her cheek into the curve of his palm, striving to memorize the sensations his touch elicited.

"Oh, Am—my lady," Lesley groaned, loosing Lucifer's rein to take her face in both his hands.

She made a sound in her throat as his mouth descended upon hers, more a mewl of protest than a moan of pleasure, but it served just as well to part her lips. The exquisite sweetness of her mouth made Lesley groan and sweep his arms around her, his embrace so fierce and sudden that Lucifer snorted

113

and shifted beneath them, his movement doing more than Lesley's to displace the rapier sheathed and belted to his waist.

"Oh!" Amanda gasped, springing stiff and wide-eyed away from him.

"Your pardon, my lady." Reclaiming the leathers, Lesley fumbled to soothe Lucifer and at the same time readjust his scabbard. " 'Tis only my rapier."

"Ohhh," Amanda responded, but it was more a moan than a sigh. "I must go!"

"My lady, please—" Lesley begged, but she was already scrambling onto her knees and reaching for the wall.

He had no choice then but to use both hands to keep Lucifer calm and steady so she didn't break her neck in the process. From the top of the wall she looked back at him, her tumbled hair gleaming from a light burning in a second-story window.

"I thank you for seeing me home," she said, her voice small and quavering. "And I wish you well, sir."

" 'Tis a pity you are a lady, my lady," Lesley replied softly, "for I think the two of us would deal very well together."

"You must not say such things!" Amanda cried, a catch in her voice. "It is most unseemly!"

"The truth is never unseemly."

"In this case it is." Biting her lower lip, she drew a deep but shaky breath. "And we must never see each other again. It's far too dangerous!"

"My lady . . ." Lesley implored, but Amanda was already scrambling up the oak tree.

Swift and sure as a monkey she climbed, yet Lesley's palms went clammy and damp on the leathers watching her shinny the length of a broad limb.

When she caught a thick branch above her and used it to swing herself into mid-air, he held his breath until she'd dropped nimbly onto a third-floor balcony. The far upper left, he noted, wiping first his left and then his right hand on his shirt front.

For a moment she stood in the thin pool of light thrown by the candles burning in the window beneath her and tentatively raised one hand. Lesley thought she meant to wave, but suddenly she pressed her fingertips to her lips, then whirled and fled inside through the French doors.

By God, she loves me, he realized, grinning at the faint click of the latch behind her. She loves me, she loves me! Amanda Gilbertson loves—

A thought so horrifying it struck him like a blow caused Lesley to jerk bolt upright in his saddle. She loved him, all right, but she loved the *wrong* him.

Chapter Twelve

The sky was just beginning to lighten when a weary and worried Andrew returned to Hanover Square. That the house lay dark and still caused him to hope Amanda was safely home and his parents snugly abed. With the aid of his exhausted coachman, he negotiated the steps and placed his key in the lock, then dismissed the man and hobbled on his swollen ankle up the steps to his sister's room.

The door was unlocked, and Andrew pushed it inward with a tiny squeak of the hinges. The first mauve streaks of dawn filtered through the balcony doors and showed him Amanda curled on her side in her bed. With a sigh of relief, Andrew limped into the room for a closer look.

She was asleep, her breathing deep and regular, her fingertips curved against her lips. There was a smile on her face, an oddly serene smile, thought Andrew, considering she'd been swooped up just hours ago and carried off on horseback by a masked man. But no matter. She was safe, hopefully unharmed, and apparently not at all overset by her ordeal.

He turned away from the bed then and hobbled off to his own chamber, his relief giving way to anger. Bright and early this day, Bow Street would hear from Viscount Welsey about Mr. Gerald Fisk. Odious little man. It went beyond the pale for a gentleman to be treated in such shabby fashion! Hours of questions put to him with only a single glass of sherry!

Removing his coat, wilted neckcloth, and shoes, Andrew undid his waistcoat and the studs at his wrists and, already three parts asleep, tumbled into bed. It seemed to him that his head had no sooner touched the pillow than he was being shaken awake.

"M'lord! M'lord, wake up!"

"Unnhhh," Andrew groaned, dimly recognizing the voice as that of Simms, his valet.

"M'lord, quickly!" Water sprinkled across his whiskered cheek and made him flinch. "There's a dreadful row downstairs, and his lordship is calling—nay, *bellowing*—for your attendance!"

"Whaaa—" Andrew groaned again, forcing himself upright, just as Lady Hampton's all-too-familiar shriek reached his ears.

It was so familiar that he yawned and fell back on his side, until his father's voice thundered, *"Andrew! Amanda!"*

He rolled off the bed then and onto his feet, gasping as a jolt of pain shot from his ankle up his calf. Wincing and hissing, with Simms beside him trying to prop him up, Andrew limped to his chamber door and flung it open. He lurched into the corridor and nearly collided with Amanda, her elbow in Marie's hand, her hair unbrushed and her wrapper untied.

"Mandy!"

"Oh, Andy!"

They hugged each other fiercely.

"Thank God you're all right!"

"Where *were* you all night? I was awake an absolute *age* waiting for you!"

"You aren't hurt or—or anything—are you?"

"Andrew Edward William Gilbertson!" Amanda said, planting a doubled fist in his chest and pushing him away. "I was brought home by a *gentleman*!"

"Who just happens to wear a black silk mask," he retorted, rubbing his breastbone. "Who in God's name *is* he?"

"I don't know," she replied truthfully, a ring of resolve in her voice. "All I know is I intend to marry him—if I can find him."

"Amanda Elizabeth Wilhe—"

"Don't even *think* to call me Wilhelmina!"

"An-*drew*!" Lord Hampton roared. "A-*manda*!"

"Oh, God, come on!"

Catching Amanda's hand, Andrew towed her down the stairs to the landing, where they had to give way to a footman climbing toward them with their prostrate mother in his arms. Backed against the wall to give him clearance, they exchanged a look of wide-eyed trepidation as a glowering Lord Hampton appeared below them in the foyer, his hands folded behind him.

"My study," he bit at them, "this instant!"

They were there in less, nipping into the chairs placed before his desk. Lord Hampton stood behind it.

"Explain how this came into the Baroness Blumfield's possession." He dropped one of Amanda's slippers onto the blotter, a sapphire blue one that matched the gown she'd worn last night. "I'd ask your mother, but as you saw, she fell into a swoon when the baroness called a short while ago and presented this in lieu of her card."

"I thought you'd put your slippers in your reticule!" Andrew flung accusingly at Amanda.

"I did!" She huffed. "It must've fallen out! Perhaps when I jumped over the terrace wall."

"So that's what tripped me! I've you to thank for nearly breaking my neck!"

"Enough!" Lord Hampton banged the slipper on the desk. "Why, miss, did you remove your shoes?"

"I don't suppose," Amanda asked haltingly, "you'd believe my feet were sore from dancing?"

"I would not."

"Very well, then," she sighed resignedly. "I took them off and put them in my reticule so Smythe wouldn't hear me creeping along behind him."

"The thief, Smythe? The one who made free with you in the Duchess of Braxton's garden?"

"No, Papa, that was the gentleman in the black mask," she corrected, a faint blush staining her cheeks.

"And where were you?" their father demanded of Andrew.

"Creeping along behind Amanda," he owned sheepishly.

"Obviously unaware," Lord Hampton retorted scathingly, "that the Baroness Blumfield was creeping along behind *you*."

Andrew cringed. "Obviously."

"The baroness gave me to understand—before I showed her the door—that you were all night at Lady Cottingham's answering questions put to you by a Mr. Fisk of Bow Street. Is that so?"

"Yes, sir. You see, Smythe tried to rob Lady Cottingham and I—"

"And where were you, miss?" Lord Hampton cut him off and wheeled on Amanda.

"I was here, Papa, asleep in my bed."

"And who escorted you home?"

"Why, Lord Earnshaw, of course," she replied, the lie falling as blithely from her lips as the truth.

"Indeed?" Lord Hampton withdrew a folded note from his coat, opened it, and read, " 'My dearest Amanda: Having given the matter of Smythe my gravest consideration, and being sufficiently recovered from my exertions of last evening, I shall call this morning upon Lord Cottingham and, if necessary, upon Bow Street, to see the scoundrel brought to justice. Again, my thanks to Welsey for seeing you safely home. Your Faithful Servant, L.E.' "

Groaning, Andrew wiped one hand over his face and sank lower in his chair. But Amanda, though she went alarmingly pale, sat straight and prim in her sleep-wrinkled night rail.

" 'Tis a sad commentary," remarked Lord Hampton, as he let the note fall beside the slipper, "that I must stoop to the Baroness Blumfield's tricks to ascertain the truth from my own children."

"I can explain, Papa," said Amanda calmly.

"What you can do, miss," he replied frostily, "is return to your room with your abigail and begin packing your cases. I am removing you to Hampton Hall until your marriage banns are posted and the ceremony arranged."

"I won't go!" Amanda stamped furiously to her feet. "And I will *not* marry Lesley Earnshaw! I *cannot*, for I love someone else!"

"You what?" Lord Hampton shrieked, the shrill in his voice uncannily like that of his countess.

"What she means, sir," Andrew inserted, leaping to his feet and into the fray before Amanda botched it further, "is that she cannot marry Lord Earnshaw because he has played her false. I saw him with my own eyes forget himself and limp on his right foot."

"Is that your only proof?" he demanded, one brow arching dubiously. "Do you think me a complete slowtop?"

"Of *course* not, sir," Andrew assured him effusively, "but the day before he limped on his left."

"And you saw that, too, with your own eyes?"

"Well, no, but Mandy assures me—"

"Exactly so." Lord Hampton snapped, glowering thunderously at his daughter. "I fear Amanda would assure the devil himself, if she thought it would free her from the match. Wouldn't you, pet?"

"I would!" Amanda declared vehemently. "And I—"

"—also overheard a conversation between two gentlemen," Andrew cut in loudly, giving Amanda a quelling look, "one of them an acquaintance of Lord Earnshaw. They were speculating on precisely where he had been wounded."

"Why—" Lord Hampton frowned thoughtfully. "I believe it was at Waterloo."

"Yes, sir, but not *that* where—if you take my meaning—the *other* where."

"Not that where but . . ." The earl went stiff as his shirt points. "Not in front of your sister!"

"Why not in front of me?" Amanda returned. "Lord Earnshaw sat on a pillow right beside me."

Lord Hampton fell in a daze into the high-backed leather chair behind his desk. "Surely *not* at Lady Cottingham's!"

"No, when he took me driving. He said leather was chilly this time of year, but it struck me odd."

"To say the least." Lord Hampton glowered

again, this time at a spot somewhere above the heads of his children, as he reviewed his interview with Earnshaw and recalled the remark that had sent him into a choking fit.

He was not so distracted, however, that the smile Amanda flicked at Andrew and the squeeze she gave his fingers went unnoticed. But he misread her thanks and gratitude for triumph and congratulation.

"I believe I have the whole of it now," he announced and came to his feet. "You're bamming me. Or trying to."

"Papa, *no!*" Amanda and Andrew cried in unison.

"Papa, *yes!* Don't think I've forgotten how, when you were children, you would defend each other, confess to the other's sins, switch the parts back and forth till I scarce knew my name! And you thought it would work again, did you? Well, have another think!" Lord Hampton banged the slipper on the desk again. "While you're packing your cases for Hampton Hall! Marie!"

"M'lord?" The study door swung inward, so suddenly that the knob, which clearly Marie had already taken hold of before the earl shouted her name, nearly slipped out of her hand and spilled her onto the carpet.

"See that Lady Amanda's trunks are packed. She's leaving for Hampton Hall on the morrow." Lord Hampton fished a key out of his waistcoat pocket and came around the desk to hand it to her. "When you've done, lock her in her chamber and post yourself outside the door."

"Yes, m'lord." She slipped the key in her apron pocket and bobbed a curtsy.

Amanda opened her mouth to howl a protest, but

Andrew stilled her with a quick shake of his head and a fingertip touched to his lips. Trusting him, as she always had, she lowered her chin docilely and moved toward the door, quite missing the wink exchanged by her brother and her abigail.

"You should thank your lucky stars you've reached your majority!" Lord Hampton seethed, once the door had shut behind Amanda and Marie. "Else I'd pack you off to my regiment this very minute!"

"Sir, if we could but discuss this calmly, as two gentlemen—"

"Oh, indeed, we shall discuss it!" his father snapped peevishly, tucking Lord Earnshaw's note in his pocket and moving toward the door. "But I doubt calmly, and not just now. I must see to your mother."

Looking flushed and harried, Lord Hampton quit the room, slamming the door behind him with such force that Andrew winced. Only once before had he seen his father this distraught, when Amanda had tumbled off her first pony and it was thought her arm might be broken. Though unlike, the situations were similar, for the emotions that had impelled Lord Hampton then—fear, worry, and a deep abiding love for his daughter—were impelling him now.

So late we grow so wise, Andrew reflected ruefully, as he limped upstairs to his rooms. He decided, while Simms made him presentable and wrapped his ankle in clean linen strips to support it, that reason must somehow be made to prevail. To that end, he went downstairs again and arrived in the foyer in time to see, through the door being shut by the butler, Lord and Lady Hampton ascending their carriage.

"Randall?" He inquired, as the coach rolled away from the gutter. "Do you know my parents' direction?"

"Bond Street, m'lord."

Not a good omen, thought Andrew, turning to balefully regard the two flights of stairs he'd just descended. He cursed every one of them as he climbed them again and knocked at Amanda's chamber. The door inched open, a brown eye beheld him through the crack, then Marie stepped back to admit him.

Portmanteaus stood open but empty on the floor, and Amanda, gowned in blue sprigged muslin with her hair brushed and held back in waves by a riband, sat glumly on her bed, her knees drawn up within the circle of her arms. Seeing him, she sprang to her feet with a hopeful smile.

"I thought you'd never come! What did Papa say? Am I still a prisoner?"

"For the moment." Andrew sighed gratefully onto the bed and propped his ankle on the chest that sat at the foot. "He and Mama have gone to the duchess."

"Oh." It was more a groan as she sank down beside him, still and pensive for a moment, until her fists balled in her lap. "Then I shall run away."

"With all this luggage?" Andrew returned, waving a hand at the trunks.

Amanda flung him a defiant glare. "I will *not* marry Lesley Earnshaw!"

"Of course you won't. I have a plan."

"Andy," she said deprecatingly, "it's plans and schemes that have landed me in this coil. I think I've had done with them for a while."

"But this one could save you," he wheedled, in a singsong voice.

Hesitating, she bit her lip, sighed, and flounced around on the bed to face him. "What must I do?"

"Play the obedient daughter, pack your cases, and let me handle the rest."

"What rest? You won't tell me?"

"I'm about to. It came to me when Papa accused us of plotting against him, which, of course, we weren't, but because he thinks we are, we might as well have a go. So I'm off to Mayfair to tell Lord Earnshaw you've a tendre for someone else and to ask him to do the gentlemanly thing."

"Oh, Andy, you're brilliant!" Amanda shot up on her knees, hugged him tightly to her bosom, then sat back on her heels and clasped his hands in her lap. "And you'll adore him, I know! He's so strong and gentle and—"

"Who?" Andrew blurted.

"Why—" Amanda cocked her head at him puzzledly "—my dearest darling."

"Your dearest—Good God!" Andrew leaped to his feet so suddenly he gave his ankle a wrench he didn't feel. "You mean *him*, don't you? The brute in the black mask!"

"He's not a brute, he's a *thief*! Of course, he can't stay one, else Papa will never receive him."

Andrew gaped at her, aghast. "You're serious!"

"I *told* you I intend to marry him," Amanda retorted. "I told Papa, too. And I intend to tell *him* once I find him."

Small as Amanda was, Andrew gauged the portmanteau would hold her easily. Not comfortably, but perhaps being bounced all the way to Hampton Hall with the rest of the luggage would jolt her back to her senses. The only flaw in it was eventually she'd have to be let out, so he discarded the notion.

Regretfully. But the moment it took him to do so allowed him to gather his wits.

"Are you certain of your feelings for this man?"

"Oh, *yes*," Amanda gushed, her eyes shining. "He's everything Lord Earnshaw isn't. Brave and honest—"

"Now there's something original—an honest thief." Andrew forced a bantering tone into his voice. "I wonder what the marriage settlement will be? The silver or Mama's jewels."

"Please don't tease, Andy," Amanda chided. "How am I going to find him?"

"Perhaps if I had his name, I could make inquiries."

"I only know the name of his horse," she replied sheepishly.

"Too bad we can't ask Smythe. Same livelihood. Bound to know one another."

"I've thought of that, and it occurs to me—"

"Don't!" Andrew leveled his index finger at her. "Just tend to the packing and let me tend to the thinking. And if Papa returns before I do, dub yer mummer about your—er—dearest darling. One hurdle at a time."

Amanda swore to keep her mummer dubbed, and Andrew ordered his bays put to his curricle. He intended to present himself in Bow Street before Mayfair and, with any luck, to Mr. Gerald Fisk. Surely Amanda's dearest darling couldn't be that hard to find. How many thieves, after all, rode the streets of London in a black silk mask?

Chapter Thirteen

How to make her love the right him, the real *him?*

The question kept Lesley awake the remainder of the night. It was a simplification, really, for Amanda did love the real him—but didn't know it—and justifiably hated the wrong him. The problem was how to switch places with himself. It confused even Lesley when he considered it in its long form, hence the simplification.

The note intercepted by Lord Hampton was the first step toward wheedling his way into Amanda's good graces. The second was ordering the removal of the horrid waistcoats to the dustbin, a task which brought a grin to the face of the normally dour Packston. He skipped over the third, the promised call on Lord Cottingham, to consider the fourth—Bow Street, Mr. Fisk, and Smythe—while Packston shaved and dressed him.

For catching up the pesky thief, Lesley decided, would do more to win Amanda's heart than anything else. It would also rid him of Fisk and free his mind to dwell on more important matters—Amanda's bride gift and where he would take her on their wedding trip. Italy, he thought, or perhaps the Greek Islands.

Once done with Bow Street, he ought to consult his man of business. No doubt there were changes Amanda would want to make here in Mayfair and at Braxton Hall to the apartment kept for him there. But no, a house of their own would be more the thing, for the children would drive Charles to distraction. Which reminded him he must take his brother to task in the matter of their mother and the family capital.

His head filled with plans, Lesley descended the stairs. He reached the foyer just as his butler opened the door to Mr. Gerald Fisk, his walking stick in one hand, his card, ready to present, in the other. He was, as he'd been the other day, dressed all in gray.

"You've saved me a trip, Fisk, for I was just on my way to see you."

"Like minds, my lord." He swept off his hat, but kept it and his stick and followed Lesley into a small parlor.

"Not feeling discreet today, eh?" He remarked jovially, as he closed the door and stepped away from it. "I'd have thought you'd present yourself in the kitchens, or at least in disguise."

"Being discreet requires time, which I'm presently in short supply of, my lord." Fisk stopped in the middle of the room, turned a half circle, and nodded at the second door in an interior wall. "I trust that leads to the back of the house and the servant's entrance?"

"It does."

"I shall be leaving that way, then, for you'll shortly be receiving another caller. I did my best to see Viscount Welsey detained, but as he kicked up

a bit of a dust at the delay, I doubt my associates
will be able to keep him long at Bow Street."

"What the devil is Welsey doing there?"

Fisk turned to face him, a smile lifting the corners of his gray eyes. "Demanding the immediate
arrest of the gentleman thief who wears a black
silk mask and rides a black stallion."

"Good God!" Lesley exclaimed increduously.

"You seem surprised, my lord. What did you expect he would do after witnessing his sister's abduction? A skillful piece of riding, by the way."

"You were there?"

"I said I would be. Deftly done, but you chose to
snatch up the wrong quarry."

"There *was* no choice," Lesley retorted sharply,
taking a menacing step toward him. "The lady is
my betrothed."

"I also have it from Welsey," Fisk replied, holding his ground, "that he and Lady Amanda were
present in your mother's garden. She was intent
then on capturing Smythe, and still is, her brother
assures me. Why in heaven's name, if you knew the
blackguard's name, didn't you *tell* me?"

"You didn't *ask* his name," Lesley shot back.
"You asked my help in catching him up. Extorted
it, rather, and it's since occured to me that there
must be a law prohibiting blackmail!"

"There *is*, my lord," Fisk snapped belligerantly.
"Just as there is a law against dueling!"

Glaring implacably at one another, they stood
nose to nose, or rather Fisk's nose to Lesley's second shirt stud, until there came a knock at the door.

"What is it, Benson?"

"The Viscount Welsey, my lord," came the butler's muffled voice through the door.

"Show him to the library. I'll join him shortly."

"Yes, my lord."

"Did you have another reason for coming?" Lesley demanded of Fisk. "If so, state it quickly."

"Only this," he answered curtly. "Brave as she may be, Lady Amanda is a distraction and a nuisance. Persuade her to leave off her reckless pursuit of Smythe, or persuade her to repair elsewhere until he is caught up. I've enough on my plate just now. And so, my lord, do you."

"Like minds again," Lesley quipped acidly, "for I intend to see one or the other accomplished by day's end."

" 'Twould be better to see Smythe in Newgate." With a brusque nod, Fisk crossed the room and looked back at Lesley with one hand on the knob. "He'd be there now if you'd nabbed him when you had the chance."

"Nabbing him is *your* job, Fisk."

"So it is." He acknowledged Lesley's parry with a slight bow. "Touché, my lord, and good day."

"It *was* a good day," Lesley muttered, striding purposefully from the parlor toward the library.

Andrew came to his feet as Lesley entered the room, feeling a touch of unease at the base of his spine at the muscle leaping in Lesley's jaw and the smolder in his eyes. He'd expected to be received by the fribble with the quizzing glass, not a Corinthian turned out in the highest kick of fashion. Had he forgotten himself again, Andrew wondered, noting the absence of his cane.

"Welsey." Lesley greeted him with a tight smile and his hand outstretched. "Good of you to call."

"I was in the neighborhood," replied Andrew, wincing at the strength in his grip. "I see you've recovered from your indisposition of last evening."

" 'Twas a momentary thing." Lesley waved him

into the leather chair he'd risen from and seated himself in its companion. "May I offer you coffee? Or a brandy, perhaps?"

"Nothing, thank you. I won't take much of your time."

"I've all day," Lesley assured him. "Did Amanda enjoy the remainder of the ball?"

"Oh, quite," Andrew lied easily, for he'd expected the question. "Danced with so many fellows I lost count."

"Excellent." Lesley leaned his elbow on the arm of his chair, made a fist, and propped his chin on his knuckles. "I'm delighted my leave taking didn't spoil her evening."

Though he smiled and seemed quite relaxed, he did not sound the least bit delighted. There was an edge in his voice and a faint yellow smear on the side of his jaw. The remnant, Andrew guessed, of a fading bruise.

"She was a bit downpin at first," he replied, "but she plucked up soon enough."

"Oh, good. I shouldn't want a wife who isn't plucky."

"That's Amanda," Andrew agreed cheerfully. "Pluck to the bone."

"Splendid. Then we shall deal very well together."

Damn the man, Andrew swore under his breath, he wasn't making this easy. Agreeable as he appeared, the curtness of his replies and the intensity of his gaze had turned Andrew's palms clammy. This was the Lord Earnshaw who'd fought two duels, he thought, wondering if he'd find himself at dawn on a foggy patch of ground with a pistol in his hand for what he was about to say. But no, he decided. This was also the Lord Earnshaw who'd played Amanda false, who no more wanted his sister than she wanted him.

"It's about Amanda that I've come, actually," he said.

"I'd assumed as much," Lesley replied, and waited, the mildness in his voice belying the agitation gnawing at him. The problem of how to straighten things out with Amanda was taking on monumental proportions, and that Welsey was about to drop another complication in his lap he had no doubt.

"It's a matter of some delicacy," Andrew went on, clasping his hands upon his crossed knees and striving to appear as calm as Lord Earnshaw. "When Amanda confided it to me, I volunteered to speak to you. It seemed a thing best discussed between gentlemen."

"Of course." Lesley nodded, noting the emphasis he gave the word gentlemen. "Then may I suggest you state it plainly."

He meant get to the point, and Andrew decided that course was best. If things went badly, he would at least have the rest of the day to round up his seconds.

"Simply, then, Amanda does not wish to marry you. She holds you in the highest regard, but she has bestowed her affections elsewhere."

"You mean she's in love with someone else?" Lesley managed, calmly enough.

"That's putting it rather baldly, my lord, but yes."

Lesley thought, rather he hoped—no, damn it to hell and back, he prayed with every fiber of his being—that Amanda was in love with the man in the black mask. But was she? That Welsey had just come from Bow Street seemed to suggest that she'd confided her lover's identity; but on the other hand, no gentleman in his right mind could possibly approve such a match, or would take it upon himself to act as go-between to bring it about.

No, no, he had the leads crossed again. If Welsey approved the liaison, he wouldn't have demanded his arrest. That seemed to point toward an unknown third party. Was there such a man, or was he merely confused again?

"It quite stunned me as well," Andrew went on, growing nervous at Lord Earnshaw's lengthy and perplexed silence. "Dashed poor timing, as her engagement to you has been announced, but I reckon the heart pays no heed to propriety. The only solution seemed to be to ask you to do the gentlemanly thing."

Lord Earnshaw's gaze had drifted away from him but swung so abruptly and fiercely back that Andrew started visibly. "Are you asking me to step aside?"

"Er"—he swallowed hard—"yes, my lord, I am."

"And what does Lord Hampton say to this?"

"I hoped—or rather, Amanda hoped—that if you agreed he would as well."

But he was not certain of it, for his eyes did not quite meet his. He could probably badger the truth out of him, but Lesley chose not to. The courage it had taken Welsey to come here and plead his sister's case deserved that much of his respect, at least. And the truth was best sought at its source.

"I have no wish to press my suit—if it is, as you say, unwanted—yet I must confess that I am devastated."

Caught flat by the revelation, Andrew sat bolt upright in his chair. His reaction told Lesley he'd come here expecting instant capitulation. The re-

alization made him feel angry—very, *very* angry—
and very perverse.

"I have told the truth, my lord," Andrew retorted
indignantly. "Do you mean to say otherwise?"

"Certainly not." Lesley laid his elbows on the
arms of his chair and laced his fingers over his
waistcoat. "For I doubt Amanda would ever forgive
me if I presented your corpse as her bride gift."

And neither would I, thought Andrew, resisting
the horrified urge he felt to clap both hands over
his mouth.

"What I mean to say is that I'm not feeling particularly gentlemanly today. Perhaps I will tomorrow." Lesley paused and shrugged. "But perhaps
not."

"Is that the answer you wish me to give
Amanda?"

"Yes." Lord Earnshaw smiled at him. "I believe
it is." It was not a particularly pleasant smile.

"But you will consider the matter?"

"I suppose I shall have to." Lesley stood and
sighed. "Although I can't promise I will."

"I see," Andrew said, but rose to his feet not at
all sure he did.

"Do drop by anytime." Hooking his hand around
Andrew's elbow, Lesley marched him double time
out of the library and into the foyer. "Always a
pleasure."

"Thank you, my lord, but—oomph!" The breath
went out of him as Lord Earnshaw swept Andrew's
curled beaver hat off a table, shoved it into his
chest, flung open the door, and pushed him outside.

"Do give Amanda my best." Lesley slammed the
door in Andrew's startled face, then sprang up the
stairs two at a time shouting for Packston.

The valet met him in the doorway of his dressing room. "Yes, m'lord?"

"The buff pantaloons and shirt I had you put in the luggage boot of the carriage last night. Where are they?"

"In the dustbin," Packston replied archly, "with the rest of the rubbish."

"Well, fetch them out," Lesley ordered curtly. "I have need of them."

This evening his mother was expecting him for supper, along with Amanda and Lord and Lady Hampton. In light of Welsey's visit, it would be a most interesting meal. But an even more interesting dessert. Picturing Amanda in a maidenly night rail, opening her balcony doors to the man in the black mask, made Lesley's pulse quicken with desire. And trepidation, for the look on her face when she beheld him would tell the tale.

The only bend in the branch was climbing the monstrous oak to reach the balcony. The thought made him queasy, but he withdrew his rapier from the scabbard hung on the back of a chair, took several practice cuts, and smiled. He always felt in top form and did his best thinking with a blade in his hand.

For Andrew, it was driving that usually helped him sort things into their proper order, but he was still not at all sure what Lord Earnshaw had said to him when he returned to Hanover Square and Marie admitted him to Amanda's bedchamber. There were several gowns wrapped in tissue on the counterpane and a row of shoes by the foot of the bed, but the portmanteaus were still empty.

"This doesn't look terribly convincing, Mandy,"

he observed as he sank into a chair near the balcony doors.

"Neither do you," she replied, putting aside the hatbox she'd just taken down from a shelf in the clothespress. "What did the beast say?"

"Beast?" Andrew said, raising an eyebrow and placing his ankle onto an embroidered footstool. "Yesterday he was only a creature."

"Andy," Amanda said threateningly.

"Well." He smiled thinly. "He didn't say no."

"But he didn't say yes."

"Truthfully, I'm not sure what he said, other than he was devastated."

"Fustian!" She sniffed, and swept across the room to rummage through the items on her dressing table.

"I believe him."

"It's a Banbury tale!" Amanda declared, wheeling to face him with the blue velvet cushion that held her pins clenched in one fist. "You saw yourself—"

"I know." Andrew held up one palm to silence her. "But if you'd seen his face when he said it, Mandy. He looked—run through."

"I'd *like* to run him through!" Amanda jabbed a stay pin into the velvet sphere with such force it went through and stabbed her. "Ouch!" She popped her finger into her mouth and dropped the cushion.

It rolled across the floor and came to rest against the leg of Andrew's chair. Frowning pensively, he leaned over to retrieve it and sat tossing it up and down.

"Why is he being so mulish?" Amanda fumed, sitting down at her table. "He doesn't want me, he contrived that ridiculous fop charade to rid himself of me, so *why* won't he step aside?"

"Perhaps he does want you," Andrew suggested thoughtfully.

"Oh, yes," she agreed, raising an ironic eyebrow, "what better reason to do everything he could think of to make me loathe him."

"But what if he connived the charade *thinking* he didn't want you," Andrew said slowly, reasoning as he went along, "and then decided he *did*?"

"I think you sprained your brain as well as your ankle," Amanda retorted and rose from the table. "If he had, why didn't he simply say so?"

"I don't know," Andrew admitted, and yawned hugely.

"Exactly." Crossing to his chair, she sat down on the arm and took the cushion away from him. "You're worn thin, Andy. Better rest a bit and leave the thinking to me."

"I can't imagine a worse place to leave it," he grumbled, the pain in his ankle making him cranky. "And you're supposed to be packing for Hampton Hall."

"I can do both," Amanda assured him, and patted his shoulder soothingly.

She'd been doing both, in fact, since Lord Hampton had banished her to her room. There was a small case under the bed she'd been slipping things into when Marie's back was turned, and a plan so mad was taking shape in her head, it even frightened her.

"I suggest prayer in lieu of thought," Andrew said, "for it will take the veriest miracle to save you from marriage to Lesley Earnshaw."

At that moment, the miracle was descending his carriage in front of the Gilbertson house, blithely unaware that he was three days late for his brother's welcome home ball.

Chapter Fourteen

The importance of the caller brought Randall him-
self up the stairs to Amanda's bedchamber.

"M'lord," he announced to Andrew when Marie
opened the door. " 'Tis the Duke of Braxton. I told
him his lordship isn't in, and that you were indisposed, but he insists—"

"Oh, God's teeth," Andrew groaned, clutching the
arms of his chair and easing his ankle gingerly to
the floor. "The stairs *again!*"

"You simply *can't* manage them," Amanda said,
her voice solicitous, but hope springing in her
breast. "I'll go down to receive Charles."

"I shouldn't let you." He wasn't at all fooled by
his sister's bland expression, but the throb in his
ankle overcame his better judgment. What harm,
he reasoned, could come from a cup of tea in the
drawing room? "Should Mama and Papa return—"

"I'll be up the stairs in a flash," Amanda assured
him. "And I can watch for them through the windows!"

Before Andrew could gainsay her, she was out
the door, down the steps, and across the foyer. She

let herself into the drawing room, hesitated for just a moment, then shut the doors behind her.

At the firm click of the latches, Charles Earnshaw turned away from the tall windows that faced the square. His hands were clasped behind him but sprang apart at the sight of Amanda, her face uncommonly flushed, standing with her back against the inlaid panels.

"Amanda, my dear! How delightful!" He started toward her with his hands outstretched, but came to an abrupt stop, a slight frown drawing his brows together. "Perhaps I've been rusticating too long, but shouldn't you leave the doors ajar?"

In his travel-rumpled coat, plainly tied cravat, and unstylishly low shirt points, His Grace looked rusticated. His dark hair was tousled from his hanging out the carriage window testing the device he'd created to measure wind speed, and at the gutter, his four-in-hand stood steaming and blowing heavily from the experiment.

"There are matters afoot more important than propriety," Amanda replied, hurrying across the room to clasp his wrists and gaze intently up into his face. "Andy said I needed a miracle, and here you are!"

"Well! I'm flattered!" The duke grinned, something he rarely did, for he was usually too deep in scholarly ruminations, and for a moment looked so like his brother Lesley that Amanda felt her breath catch. "I've been called many things, but never miraculous."

"You are my dearest friend, Charles, and I'm in desperate need of one just now. Will you help me?"

"If I can, of course, though I can't imagine how I—"

Amanda tugged him so abruptly down on a near-at-hand settee that the Duke of Braxton stumbled and all but fell onto it beside her. Drawing a deep breath, she announced, "I am betrothed to Lesley."

"Are you? Then I wish you happy!" His Grace beamed at her. "Lesley who?"

"Charles." Amanda spoke his name patiently. "Your *brother* Lesley."

"No, really? Well, capital! We shall be able to correspond now without all that silliness of sending letters through Andrew. How is he, by the way? Randall said he was indisposed."

"He's only sprained his ankle. It's why he didn't come down. Now Charles—"

"I feel badly asking for him, then. I don't usually insist, don't like to, you know, though actually I called to see you. I thought Andrew could fix it, and I suppose he has, in an odd way. And now you tell me you're to be my sister-in-law. How marvelous!" Charles paused and frowned puzzledly. "I wonder why Mother didn't write it in the note she sent asking me to come up for Lesley's welcome home ball? Hmmm." He shrugged it off and brightened. "Will you announce your engagement then?"

Though she wanted to shriek at him, pressed as she was for time and a solution, Amanda restrained herself. When he wasn't discoursing on science or literature, Charles had a tendancy to ramble, and it was best, within reason, to let him do so.

"Lesley's welcome home ball," she told him simply, for it was the best way, "was three days ago."

"I've missed it then! Drat!" He rapped his knuckles impatiently against his knee. "Did I miss the announcement of your engagement, as well?"

"It's only been in the papers," Amanda replied, taking his hands and holding them tightly in hers, "and it's what I need your help with, Charles."

"Oh, dear," he said, flushing, and then frowning. "I'm no good with that sort of thing. Ask my mother."

"Oh, Charles!" Amanda cried excitedly, gripping his hands so tightly he winced. "I knew your great mind would think of something! It's perfectly brilliant! And after all, you *are* head of the family!"

"I am?" His Grace querried blankly. "Oh—yes, I am, I suppose. I keep forgetting that, you see, for it gives Mother such pleasure to believe *she* is. And, poor dear, she has so little else to do that I—"

"But she'll listen to you, Charles," Amanda interrupted, "for she is only a woman, and *must* bow to your wishes. As *I* must bow to Papa's wishes. And don't you see? If *you* forbid the match, then Her Grace—"

"Me?" He blurted. "Why on earth would I do that?"

"For me, Charles," Amanda said, her fingers clinging imploringly to his.

"For you?" The duke repeated, looking bewildered. "You mean you don't want to marry Lesley?"

"No, I do not."

"Oh," he said, looking crestfallen. "I thought, or rather, I hoped . . . Are you *sure*? He's something of a scamp, I know, and though I haven't seen him since he's come home, Mother wrote me the war has quite changed him and—oh, dear, Amanda, are you absolutely *certain*?"

"I am," she replied firmly, seizing his comment, "for the war *has* quite changed him."

"How do you mean?"

There wasn't time for elaborate explanations, Amanda rationalized, and Captain Lord Lesley Earnshaw had no one but himself to thank for what she was about to say. Later, she could explain it all to Charles and make him understand.

"You do know he was wounded in Brussels?"

"Why, yes. Mother wrote me."

"Did she tell you where he'd been wounded?"

" 'Twas Waterloo, I believe."

"Yes, Charles. But not *that* where, the *other* where."

"Not that where, but—Oh!" The duke flushed vermillion. "Er—no. Mother didn't impart that. Nor did Lesley, as I recall, and one doesn't ask."

"*This* one did," Amanda confessed, "when he came to take me driving and he sat upon a cushion in his curricle."

"Well, you know, leather can be somewhat chill—"

"Yes, Charles, but last eve at Lady Cottingham's, I overheard two ladies commiserating my betrothal to what was *left* of Eugenia Earnshaw's son. 'Twas a pity, they said, for Lesley quite reminded them of your father—*before* he went to war."

"Before he went—" he repeated perplexedly, then suddenly blanched and sprang to his feet. "Good God! *That's* what Mother meant! Have you told Lord Hampton?"

"Some of it, yes," Amanda hedged, "but to no avail. Papa is determined to see me married."

"But surely not to such a—er—my brother!"

Amanda nodded gravely.

"And my mother?"

"Her Grace is equally set on the marriage."

"I shouldn't wonder," he muttered, his eyes, which tended more to green than Lesley's, narrowing with displeasure. "But this is monstrous! I shall forbid it!"

"Oh, thank you," Amanda sighed gratefully.

"Hmmm, but wait. There may be a bit of a snag."

"Charles, I haven't time for a snag," she urged, her gaze catching on the ormolu clock ticking on the mantle. "Papa and Mama could return at any moment. And I'm being sent to Hampton Hall first thing on the morrow."

"Well, that's it, then!" Charles exclaimed, a brilliant smile breaking over his features. "They can't have a wedding without a bride!"

"Yes, Charles. I mean—no, Charles, but—"

"Here's the thing." He sat beside her again and clasped her fingers. "Believing as she does—rather, as I have allowed her to believe—that *she* is head of the family, I fear I could forbid till I turn blue and Mother will pay me no heed. So. What we must do is prove that *I* am the duke, a person to be reckoned with, and that you cannot be bullied about."

"But how?"

"You're being removed to Hampton Hall where you can be kept under watch, and if necessary, lock and key, are you not?"

"Yes. That's Papa's thought, I'm sure."

"Well, then, removed you shall be," he announced triumphantly, "but in *my* protection. And if necessary, under my lock and key, for I shall not return you until your father and my mother agree to call off the wedding!"

"Oh, Charles," Amanda breathed admiringly, her vow to swear off plans and schemes abruptly forgotten, "you *are* a genius!"

"Yes, I know," he agreed matter-of-factly, then went on consideringly, "My father's hunting box should do nicely to hide you. Mother's forgotten the place, I'm sure, and the caretaker's wife will be there to act as chaperone. I shall have to hire a carriage, of course—mine could be recognized—I can do that this afternoon. No need to make an excuse to Mother, quite forgot to write her I was coming to town, you know. Hmmm . . . Now, how to get you out of here?"

"Oh, that's simple. I shall climb down the oak tree behind the house."

"Splendid. Then I shall collect you at—say, eleven this evening? Will Lord and Lady Hampton have retired by then?"

"No, but they'll be dining with Her Grace. I'm to be there as well, but under the circumstances, Papa may not let me attend." Amanda smiled slyly. "Especially if I throw a tantrum."

"Then be sure to throw one." The duke slapped his hands on his knees. "Anything we've forgotten?"

She thought a moment, then shook her head. "I don't think so."

"Then I shall take my leave, for there's much to do."

Charles rose, assisted Amanda to her feet, and followed her from the drawing room to the foyer. He had no beaver to claim from Randall or a footman, for he believed the wearing of hats caused one's hair to fall out. It was one of his less bizarre theories, but was nonetheless in large part the reason the fashion conscious *ton* had dubbed him His Dottiness. He paused at the door with one hand on the knob to smile fondly at Amanda.

"I should be thanking you, my dear."

"Why, Charles, whatever for?"

"For awakening me to my responsibilities and the dire consequences of allowing my mother free rein. And also," he added, with a hint of a grin, "for giving me the opportunity to get a bit of my own back from Lesley."

"You don't feel like a traitor?"

"Good heavens, no!" Charles gave a short laugh. "For all the times Lesley soaped the lenses of my reading spectacles or blacked out words in my books, this is the very *least* he deserves!"

"My thought exactly," Amanda agreed with a smile.

"Remember now." Charles lowered his voice and winked as he opened the door and stepped outside. "Eleven sharp, beneath the oak tree."

"Eleven sharp," Amanda repeated with a nod.

Sighing relievedly, she closed the door behind Charles, leaned her forehead against the cool wood, and listened to his carriage roll away down the square. Thank heaven she wouldn't have to run away alone as she'd been planning. She had but to finish packing her secret case, stage a tantrum for her father . . . and think of how best to go about finding her dearest darling.

Perhaps Tattersall's could tell her something about a black stallion named Lucifer, she thought, then started at the sound of a carriage rattling to a stop before the house. Two at a time, Amanda sprang up the steps with her skirts hiked to her knees.

In her wake, the footman hired that morning stepped out of an alcove behind the stairs. The glimpse he had of her delicate ankles brought a grin so broad to his face it bent the tip of the fake nose he'd puttied over his own.

What a sweet little ladyship she was, first to tell him her name and now to serve him the Duke of Braxton on a silver platter. Bit long in the tooth he was for her, but Quality was odd that way. And here he'd thought she'd taken a fancy to that upstart devil in the black mask.

Mayhap her little ladyship couldn't lead him to him like he'd thought, but the Dowager would pay thrice what the wretch had taken from him. And he'd find him yet, he would, just to settle the score.

"Eleven sharp, eh?" Smythe chuckled, and pinched his disguise back into shape.

Chapter Fifteen

"*Are you perchance feverish?*" The duchess demanded of Lesley, as he leaned to kiss her. "It's barely nine of the clock!"

"I'm practicing," he replied, touching his lips to her smooth brow, "for I do not wish to be late to my wedding."

"Indeed?" Her Grace remarked, nonplussed. "So you are reconciled to it?"

"Oh, quite." Lesley moved to the window and looked out at the street; he felt nervous yet excited, wondering what color gown Amanda would wear, how she would dress her hair. "She's charming, really. I believe we'll get on very well together."

"I've known that all along," his mother replied archly, "for you are alike as two peas shelled from the same pod."

"What a charming simile." Lesley grinned at her. "Have you always thought me a vegetable?"

"Only when you do witless things like adopt a cane and then neglect to lean upon it," the duchess sniffed. "Did you think to elicit Amanda's pity or her disgust?"

"The latter, actually," he admitted, "but I failed."

For she held him in utter loathing rather than mere disgust; but he would rectify that at midnight, he vowed, and drew back the drape in time to see Lord and Lady Hampton descend their carriage. A footman shut the coach behind them, and Lesley frowned, watching the lamplight gleam on the hem of the countess's gown as her husband led her across the flagway.

"You did include Amanda in your invitation, Mother?"

"Of course I did. What a silly question." But a moment later, when Denham announced the Gilbertsons and they entered the drawing room sans their daughter, she blurted, "Where is Amanda?"

"Regrettably indisposed," said her father. "She sends her sincerest apologies, Eugenia. And her best wishes to you, my lord."

Lesley knew better, but kept his voice neutral as he moved away from the window. "I trust it's nothing serious."

"Mostly bride's nerves, I suspect," Lord Hampton responded easily.

And smoothly enough, Lesley supposed, but Lady Hampton, whom he'd not seen in a number of years, flushed to the roots of her rich brown hair as Lord Hampton presented him. Her fingers trembled, and when he straightened from bowing over her hand, her head was tilted at an angle which suggested she'd been trying to peer behind him.

"Dear Hampton believes a turn in the country would be just the thing for Amanda," she said nervously, unable to decide who or what to fix her gaze upon.

"It'll pluck her up in no time, I'm sure," Lord Hampton agreed.

Still smoothly, but the word pluck and the toothsome smile that "dear Hampton" gave him roused Lesley's suspicions.

"You're sending Amanda to Hampton Hall, then?"

"Bright and early on the morrow."

"I should like to see her beforehand. How early?"

"*Very* early," Lord Hampton emphasized, then added under his breath, "Later, over our brandy, eh?"

No, *now* if you please, Lesley thought to demand, but Denham appeared to announce supper, and he was called upon to escort Lady Hampton while the earl squired his mother to the dining room. It was best to be agreeable, he decided, since he might have to call upon Lord Hampton to intercede on his behalf with Amanda. So he strove to be charming and not to appear agitated—though he was—during the parade of courses laid before him.

"We rather thought to see Charles this evening," Lady Hampton commented, once the meal was done and Lesley rose to assist her.

"Why in heaven's name," his mother queried, "did you expect to see Charles?"

"Randall said he called this afternoon while we were he—er—out," Lord Hampton hastily corrected himself. "I thought it odd Andrew didn't mention it before he left this evening. Or that Charles didn't leave his card."

"He forgets to carry them," the duchess explained, glancing worriedly at Lesley. "Do you suppose he's gotten lost again?"

"Charles is never lost, Mother," he replied bemusedly. "Bewildered, perhaps, but—"

"Oh, Bennett!" Lady Hampton said on a sharply indrawn breath. "I'll wager *that* is why Amanda was in such a pout! Marie must have told her Charles called, or mayhap she was listening at the keyhole! She does that, you know, when you lock her in—"

"Oh *my*, Cornelia," Her Grace cut in, "is that a spot on your gown?"

"Is it?" The countess looked down her nose at her bodice. "Oh dear!"

"The brandy is in the library, Lesley." His mother swiftly lifted Lady Hampton's elbow from his hand. "Do pour some for Lord Hampton. Come along, Cornelia."

Still peering at the front of her gown, the countess stumbled along behind her as the duchess all but dragged her from the room, and Lesley faced his flustered father-in-law to be.

"I take it Amanda is not in your favor."

"Well—no," he admitted. "I suggested she rest this afternoon, looked a bit wan, I thought, and I'm—er—rather afraid I had to insist."

"You don't think missing Charles's call overset her?"

"Oh, no, nothing of the sort," Lord Hampton replied jovially, but his gaze shifted fractionally. "Can't think why it would."

Unfortunately, Lesley could.

"If you'll excuse me, my lord." He made a slight bow. "I'm sure you can find your way to the library."

Turning sharply on one heel, he quit the dining room and his mother's house, noting as he strode along purposefully that it was nearly the stroke of eleven. He had an uncanny feeling time was of the essence, and regretted his decision not to stow his breeches, shirt, rapier, and Teddy's mask in the carriage, and have Tom follow along with Lucifer as he'd done the night before. To make up for it, he climbed into the box and took the reins from Reston.

While Lesley drove at breakneck speed toward Mayfair, Amanda paused on the balcony to look back at the note she'd pinned to her pillow. She was not so heartless to leave without a word and hoped her father would not blame Marie, who was fast asleep in a comfortable chair in the corridor when last she'd peeped through the keyhole.

Closing the French doors without a sound, Amanda moved to the railing and looked down into the garden. The Duke of Braxton stood beside a coachman who was holding a half-hooded lantern, which threw light enough to show Charles motioning for her case. She tossed it to him, then tucked her skirts in her waist sash, climbed onto the rail, and moved into the tree.

Just as Lesley reached Mayfair and sprang from the box into the house, shouting for Packston and for Tom to saddle Lucifer, Amanda dropped from the lowest branch of the oak onto the top of the wall. Charles was there to help her down and into the hired carriage. It smelled musty, but in the dim glow of the coachman's lantern, appeared reasonably clean.

"Let's be off, then," Charles said in a low voice to the driver.

"Right you are, Mr. Smith, sir." He nodded, removed the steps and shut the door.

"Mr. Smith?" Amanda queried with a raised brow.

"I could scarce use my title or my name," Charles replied with a grin, "so we are in disguise."

And so was Lesley by then, leaping onto Lucifer's back with only a mild curse at his abrupt landing in the saddle. The stallion burst out of the yard at a dead run, his hooves striking sparks on the cobbles, just as a closed hackney rolled out of an alleyway near the Gilbertson house and fell in behind the hired coach.

The clock in the duchess's drawing room was just striking the quarter hour when Lesley reined Lucifer so sharply next to the capped brick wall that the stallion snorted and sat back on his haunches. The faint light burning in Amanda's room gave him courage, despite the rattle of the uppermost branches of the oak tree in the stiff wind that had risen. A handful of leaves sifted earthward, one or two snagging in Lucifer's mane as Lesley kicked his right foot free of the stirrup and swung his leg to the stallion's left side.

"Wait right here, old boy." He patted Lucifer's muscled neck and reached for the wall. "If I fall, do at least please try to catch me."

The stallion snorted again and laid back his ears, but otherwise stood motionless as Lesley gained the top of the wall, left his rapier there, and started up the tree. Fixing on the light, he climbed toward it, slipping only twice on the long way up. His heart banging, he dropped onto the balcony, wiped his clammy palms on his shirt, and rapped lightly on the French doors.

There was no response. He rapped again, a bit louder, and waited what he thought was ample time for Amanda to don a wrapper before trying the handle. It turned easily in his hand, and he eased the door inward to behold the shambles she'd left in the wake of her packing.

Portmanteaus stood open but empty, gowns were

thrown upon the chairs, shoes littered the floor, but there was no sign of Amanda. A candle burned on the table beside the bed, the shadow of the flame flickering on the square of paper pinned to the pillows. Slipping noiselessly past the door, Lesley crossed the room, snatched it up, and read: 'Dearest Mama and Papa, I have chosen this course, for you leave me no other. I cannot marry Lord Earnshaw, for I love someone else. Do not worry, for I shall be safe with Charles. Your disobedient but loving daughter, Amanda.'

Lesley's first impulse was to crush the note in his fist, but he replaced it on the pillow. The linens smelled like the lavender soap Amanda used on her hair.

So she'd be safe with Charles . . . and *married* to him by morning unless he could stop them. And he would, if he could, for this was no way to become a duchess. Why in blazes hadn't Welsey told him it was Charles she loved?

Would he take her to Gretna, or would he have a special license? The latter, Lesley decided, for Charles loathed the cold and damp of Scotland. Slipping back onto the balcony and closing the French doors, he used the rail to lever himself into the tree, and tried to decide, as he climbed down, where Charles would take her.

Braxton Hall was out of the question . . . he doubted his brother had even the faintest idea where the lesser Earnshaw estates were located . . . ah, their father's hunting box. Of course! It was the perfect place to hide themselves until the scandal of their elopement was forgotten.

He'd considered taking Amanda there himself, Lesley thought bitterly, but pushed the thought aside as he dropped from the tree to the wall and from there to his saddle. Refastening his rapier at his waist, he gauged the quickest route out of the city and dug his heels into Lucifer's flanks.

No more than twenty minutes ahead, the carriage bearing Amanda and Charles was moving at a leisurely pace through the outskirts of London. The open road lay ahead, a thin gray ribbon silvered by the moon, the city behind them a dark smudge against the night.

As the coachman shifted in the box, he caught sight of the hackney trotting along in their wake. He goaded his team with a single lash, looked again and saw the smaller conveyance keeping pace. He noticed too, in a bright patch of moonlight, the well-bred look of the horses pulling it. Frowning, he rapped the floor of the box to draw Charles's attention.

When he leaned out the window, his hair blown back by the rushing wind, the driver shouted, "We're bein' followed!"

Craning his neck to look, Charles saw, by the gleam of the coach lamps, the hackney bearing down on them with its own lamps unlit. Highly suspicious, he thought, as well as highly dangerous.

"What is it, Charles?" Amanda rose on her knees on the banquette to poke her head outside. "Highwaymen?"

"In a hackney? Doubtful." Charles twisted around to shout at the driver, "Can we outrun them?"

"We c'n try, Mr. Smith!" He laid the whip to his team, and the chase was on.

The coach horses gave it their best, but they were bred for endurance not speed. Amanda and Charles (wishing he had his wind device with him), bobbed out the window, watching the hackney swing out from behind them and draw effortlessly alongside.

And ever closer, Charles noticed, as the wheels, their spokes a blur in the moonlight, inched nearer. They mean to force us off the road, he realized, and glanced at Amanda, her hair streaming around her small, heart-shaped face. Praying their pursuers were only highwaymen, he bellowed at the coachman, "Faster!"

The lash cracked, the carriage leaped ahead, and the hackney nudged closer. Aware now of the intent, the coachman flailed his whip at the box, but the other driver did not yield. He crowded even closer, bumping the carriage as the two coaches plunged in tandem over the crest of a low hill. The jolt caused the team to break stride, and sent Amanda tumbling backward on the banquette.

"Enough!" Charles shouted, springing from his seat to catch her. "Pull over!"

With his horses off stride, the coachmen had little choice but to pull back on the leads and ease them onto the verge. The driver of the hackney cut his own horses in front of the carriage, threw back his cape, and leaped from the box. He pulled a pistol from his waistband, the barrel gleaming a dull blue black in the flicker of the coachlamps.

"Be still and keep down," Charles whispered to Amanda, and kicked the door open.

He jumped to the ground, drew himself straight and declared imperiously, "You, sir, are a madman!"

"And good evenin' t'you, Yer Grace." The hackney driver bowed, then wheeled on the coachman. "Git down 'ere."

I know that voice, Amanda realized, and sprang into the open doorway behind Charles. "Smythe!"

"Evenin', yer little ladyship." He nodded to her, then turned to the coachman as he climbed down from the box. "This is fer whippin' me." He brought the pistol down sharply on the side of his head, and the driver crumpled.

"You *beast*!" Amanda shrieked.

"You *know* this reprobate?" Charles muttered over his shoulder.

"Yes," she whispered angrily. "His name is Smythe and he's a thief. He usually has two accomplices—"

"Damnit, 'Arry!" came Jack's muffled voice from inside the hackney. "Git *off* me!"

"I'm—oompf!—tryin' Jack!"

Swearing under his breath and aiming his pistol at Charles's breastbone, Smythe backed to the hackney and fumbled behind him for the latch. He found it, tripped it, and flung open the door to reveal Jack and Harry in a tumble on the floor.

"What in bloody hell 'er you doin' down there?" Smythe yelled furiously. "Yer s'posed t'have the ropes out an' be trussin' these two up!"

"Might 'elp if ye'd tell a cove you was gonna throw on the brake s'bloody quick!" Jack panted from beneath Harry. "Git this oaf offa me, will ya?"

Keeping one eye and the pistol on Charles, Smythe held out his free hand. Jack grasped it and grunted, Smythe pulled and cursed, while Harry, turned on his back like a turtle on its shell, tried to roll himself over.

The barrel of the pistol wavered, and so did Smythe's attention. Seizing the opportunity, Charles whispered to Amanda, "Get down," then reached behind him to catch the edge of the door.

She ducked, and he gathered himself to spring,

just as the pistol steadied, and Smythe's gaze swung back to him.

"I wouldn't, Yer Grace." He drew back the hammer with a click. "I doubt yer ma 'ud pay much to get y'back with a hole in yer chest."

"So that's your game," Charles remarked derisively. "Kidnapping and ransom."

"Aye." Smythe gave a final tug and Jack tumbled onto the ground with a grunt. "Git up an' git the ropes." He gave him a kick, and as Jack scrambled to his feet, he smiled at Charles. "Clever, ain't it?"

"My father," Amanda declared, popping up defiantly behind the duke, "won't pay a single farthing for me!"

But he might, she thought, after hearing she'd not only run away but managed to get herself kidnapped in the process, pay any amount Smythe demanded if he promised *not* to return her.

"Never thought t'ransom you, m'lady," Smythe told her. "It's 'Is Grace what'll fetch the blunt. Yer just along to cook fer us."

"I can't cook!" Amanda retorted indignantly. "I'm a lady!"

With a loop of stout rope over his arm, Jack was starting toward them. Harry, rubbing the back of his head, was lumbering out of the hackney. They bumped into each other, and then into Smythe.

"You damned loobies!" he shouted, grabbing Harry's shoulder and pushing him forward. "Tie up the coachman first before he comes round!"

"A sad lot, aren't they?" Amanda whispered to Charles.

"Mmmm," he agreed, wondering how best to use Harry's ineptness to their advantage. "Where do you mean to take us?"

"To yer old dad's hunting box," Smythe replied.

"How do you know our plans?" Amanda demanded.

"I was listenin' through the door, m'lady. Got meself hired as footman this mornin' by your Randall. Seemed the smart way t'find yer friend in the black mask, since ever' time I see you, I end up seein' 'im, an' 'e ends up with *my* loot."

"*Our* loot, y'mean." Jack straightened beside the coachman's prostrate form to glare at him.

" 'Course it's *our* loot," Smythe snapped at him, then grinned smugly at Amanda. "Pity your masked friend ain't here now, ain't it?"

"What masked friend?" Charles inquired of her increduously, just as Harry, squatting beside Jack and the coachman, raised his head to ask, "Is it thunderin'?"

"No, y'great twit!" Jack cuffed him on the ear. "It ain't thunder, it's—"

He heard it then, a low, pounding rumble, and flung a wide-eyed look at the rise behind them. Smythe and Charles heard it, and so did Amanda, placing her hands on his shoulders to look up the hill. She'd no sooner leaned forward than Lucifer, his sweat-lathered hide gleaming in the moonlight, plunged over the crest at an all out gallop.

"Holy Jesus!" Jack howled. "It's him!"

There was nowhere to run to in the open-ended triangle formed by the drawn together coaches but the hedgerow alongside the road. Jack made a leap for it just as Harry did. They crashed together and fell side by side, knocked senseless.

"Oh, it *is* him!" Amanda cried joyously. "My dearest darling!"

Over the pounding of Lucifer's hooves, Lesley heard her voice, but couldn't make out the words or see where she was. He had eyes only for the pistol in Smythe's hand as it swung toward him.

"Good God! That's Lucifer!" Charles gasped, and threw himself at the thief.

Behind him, Amanda screamed and threw her reticule. It sailed toward Smythe, hanging in the air for a moment along with the ring of her voice and the ring of steel as Lesley drew his rapier. The pistol fired, belching fire and smoke, a half second before her reticule and Charles both struck Smythe.

Recoiling at the shattering report, Amanda cringed and flung her hands over her eyes. She was too terrified to look until she heard Lucifer whinney, and Charles laugh, and slowly lowered her hands.

With the tip of Lesley's rapier quivering in the hollow of his throat, Smythe was pinned, arms out flung, against the side of the hackney. Sweat glistened on his face in the glow of the carriage lamps, Lucifer's hide shimmered a wet, dark blue, and Charles's teeth gleamed white in his dirty face as he got up with Smythe's pistol in his hand and brushed his soiled waistcoat.

"Nicely done," he said, grinning up at his younger brother.

"I trust you know how to use a pistol?" Lesley asked him frostily.

"Of course I do," Charles retorted indignantly. "Now look here—"

He broke off at the sound of horse's hooves, and looked back at the medium-sized sorrel galloping toward them over the hill. Lesley glanced behind him, keeping the rapier taut against Smythe's jugular, and cursed. He didn't see Amanda, who'd gone limp with relief with one hand pressed to her throat in the shawdowed door frame of the carriage.

"So you nabbed him after all, my lord!" Fisk said with a laugh, as he reined in his horse beside Lucifer.

"My lord?" Amanda gasped, her fingers sliding away from her throat.

Lesley saw her then, and felt his heart lurch between his ribs. Dirt smudged her nose, and her windblown hair tangled around her face much as it had the night he'd met her in his mother's garden.

"He's all yours, Fisk," he said brusquely and withdrew his rapier from Smythe's throat.

As the thief sagged to the ground with a moan of relief, and Fisk dismounted to take charge, Lesley wheeled Lucifer toward the carriage. A tremulous smile quivered on Amanda's lips, and his heart lurched again as he touched the blade to the tip of his nose.

"I wish you happy, my lady." He saluted her, then dug his heels into Lucifer's flanks.

"No, wait!" Amanda cried, springing up in the doorway. "Oh, please, you don't understand!"

But it was too late. Lucifer was already disappearing over the hill in a gray swirl of dust.

"I say, Lesley!" Charles strode into the middle of the road and shouted angrily after him, "How incredibly rude!"

"*What* did you say?" Thunderstruck, Amanda clutched the door frame to keep from falling.

"I said, how incredibly rude! But perhaps I should have said how insufferably—"

"No, Charles, his *name*!" she shrieked. "Who *is* he?"

"Who *is* he?" The duke eyed her increduously. "For God's sake, Amanda! Don't you know your own fiancé?"

"That was Lesley?" She squeaked, feeling suddenly faint.

"Yes, of course, it was Lesley! I admit I recognized Lucifer first, probably because he wasn't wearing a mask, but—"

"Oh no," Amanda moaned.

And then she swooned.

Chapter Sixteen

"Listen to this, Mandy." Andrew folded the morning Times in half and read, " 'It is rumored that His Highness plans to privately receive the Duke of Braxton and Lady Amanda Gilbertson to congratulate them on their daring capture of the thief Smythe and his cohorts. This is an honor most deserved by these two noble heroes.' " He gave a short laugh and grinned at his sister. "D'you suppose the pun was intentional?"

Amanda's only reply was an indifferent shrug. Still abed in her night rail and wrapper, she sat propped on her pillows staring gloomily at the cup of morning chocolate turning cold on the tray placed over her lap.

"I don't think I care much for lovesickness." Andrew tossed the paper on the floor and pulled his chair closer to the bed. "You had more to say when last you had a putrid throat."

"I should have *known*," Amanda murmured, almost to herself. "I keep going over it in my mind and it seems so clear to me now I can't think why I didn't."

"That's hindsight for you," Andrew replied philosophically, propping his nearly healed ankle on the foot of her bed.

"But it was right there for all the world and his wife to see! I suppose it's understandable I didn't connect him to the man in the black mask when he jumped Lucifer over the wall, but I *should* have at Lady Cottingham's when he appeared within an hour of his own leave taking. Especially because—"

"Are you going to drink that chocolate?"

"Do you mind awfully?" Amanda snapped irritably. "I'm trying to make sense of this."

"It's a shame to let it waste."

"Then by all means drink it."

"Thank you." Andrew helped himself to a healthy swallow. "It's my opinion you aren't trying to make sense of anything. You're just wallowing in self-pity."

"I am *not*!" Amanda declared, but a telltale flush crept up her throat.

"You are, too. It's all you've done these last two days. When are you going to get on with it?"

"Get on with what? My life?" She made a derisive noise in her throat. "It's over! I might as well don my caps!"

"You could do that." Andrew nodded. "Or you could at least make an attempt to find your dearest darling."

"What would you have me do?" Amanda folded her arms and glared at him. "No one's seen him since he galloped off on Lucifer!"

"Well." He paused to take another sip of the tepid chocolate. "Getting out of bed might be a good place to start the search."

"I don't want to get out of bed," she replied petulantly. "I've nothing to get out of bed for."

"You've got your costume to ready for the duchess's masquerade tonight, don't you?"

"I'm not going."

"You have to go, Mandy, it's in your honor. Yours and Charles's."

"Don't even mention Charles!" Amanda pushed the tray aside and angrily punched her pillows. "I haven't seen him, either, since he and Mr. Fisk brought me home and explained things to Papa!"

"And isn't that a marvel?" Andrew said brightly, looking for ways to cheer her without tipping his hand. "He's so proud, he hasn't even thought to punish you. And Mama hasn't swooned in two days!"

Amanda looked down her nose at him and glowered.

"Oh, come, Mandy. It's hardly Charles's fault Lesley thought you were eloping with him. I would have thought the same thing."

"Then you're just as totty-headed as he is!"

The flush had spread across her cheeks now, and there was a definite spark in her eyes. And she'd withdrawn one leg from under the covers.

"Perhaps," he suggested carefully, "Charles has gone looking for him."

"Or perhaps he's just driving around the countryside testing his wind device!" Amanda waved one hand above her head, then demanded increduously of her brother, "Do you know that's all he talked about on our way back to London?"

"I thought you sobbed and cried the whole story to him. Isn't that why he summoned Teddy home, to get to the bottom of things?"

"Ooh, that little jacaanapes!" Flinging the bedclothes aside, she folded her legs beneath her and clenched her fists on her knees. "This is all *his* fault!"

"Hardly, Mandy," Andrew replied reasonably. "Teddy certainly began it, but you and Lesley had an equal hand in the finish."

That should have launched her to her feet like a cannon shot, but instead she sighed heavily and sank back against the pillows.

"You're right, of course," she agreed dismally.

The spark faded from her eyes, and her toes inched toward the covers again. Oh, no you don't, Andrew thought, but was saved from flinging the linens aside and throwing her over his shoulder by a knock at the door.

"Come in," Amanda sighed again.

It was Marie, praise God, with the promised delivery from Charles.

"This just come from His Grace," she said, cleverly carrying the box to the chair farthest from the bed.

Which left Amanda no choice but to get up and cross the room to see what it was. As she pulled off the note fixed to the lid and opened it, Marie placed herself between her mistress and the bed, prepared to prevent her, bodily if necessary, from climbing back into it.

" 'My dear Amanda,' " she read aloud, " 'I've taken the liberty of arranging our costumes for the masquerade this evening. Since we are to be the honored couple, I thought we should look the part. My mother and yours kindly assisted, and I have their assurance the gown and slippers will fit. We shall be the talk of the town, I'm sure. Your devoted, Charles.' " Amanda put the note aside and looked curiously at Andrew. "Why did Mama say nothing of this to me?"

"Because she and Her Grace wanted to surprise you," he said, keeping to himself that Lord Hampton had kept his wife otherwise occupied to prevent her emptying her budget to Amanda. "Go on, open it."

"Oh my!" She breathed, as she removed the lid, tossed it aside, and lifted a filmy white gown with twists of gold in the sleeves and the bodice out of its tissue.

It was a lovely thing, even to Andrew, who knew nothing of women's clothes. At the sparkle that came into his sister's eyes as she held it against her, he glanced at Marie and winked.

"What's this?" Amanda draped the gown carefully over the back of the chair and withdrew from the bottom of the box a delicate string of golden coins.

"It's a girdle, m'lady," said Marie, coming forward to take it from her. "Goes round you like this."

"It's Roman, then." Amanda raised a dubious eyebrow as Marie roped the coins around her. "You knew about this?"

"Had to, didn't I," she replied guilelessly, "since I'm the one who dresses you. Should be something for your hair, too."

There was, a thin gold circlet, which drew another gasp from Amanda, and smoothed the suspicious pucker from her brow. As she went scurrying to her glass to admire it, Andrew breathed a sigh of relief.

"She'll be right as a trivet now," Marie murmured, patting his arm as she went to help Amanda with the circlet.

Andrew left, and quickly made his way downstairs. At the sound of his footsteps in the foyer, the study door sprang open, and Lord Hampton appeared in the threshold.

"Yes?"

"Yes." Andrew smiled.

"That's one hurdle," his father sighed. "Now if Charles can pull off the rest—"

"Don't even think that he can't," Andrew interrupted feelingly, "or we may never get her out of bed again."

"What costume did he send, by the way?"

"A gown in the Roman style."

"Good God!" Lord Hampton's eyebrows shot up his forehead. "I shudder to think what Charles will wear!"

He brows took a similar leap that evening, when the Duke of Braxton, resplendant in a toga and crown of laurel leaves, strode regally across the foyer of his mother's house to greet them. Even Andrew suffered a moment's shock behind his mask, but Amanda laughed, lightly and gaily, for the first time in two days.

"Charles, you look marvelous!"

"I do, don't I?" He grinned, tripping over the hem as he turned a circle in front of her. "But how on earth do you walk in a skirt?"

"Very carefully, Charles. Now tell me who we are."

"Because everyone is crying us heroes, who better to be, I thought, than Caesar and Calpurnia?"

"Then so we shall be." Amanda gave her cloak to a footman and took the duke's arm.

Her filmy Roman gown shimmered in the glow of the chandelier, and the girdle of coins tinkled like small bells. As the Emperor of the Tiber led his Empress away, he glanced a quick nod to the Gilbertsons over his shoulder.

"At last," Lady Hampton remarked, "I understand why everyone calls Charles His Dottiness."

"At *last*," Lord Hampton sighed, then whispered to his son, "D'you suppose that means he's done it?"

"Let us hope," Andrew muttered, and as yeoman to his Lord and Lady of the Manor parents, followed them into the ballroom.

He thought to catch Charles alone, but the crush was even worse than at Lady Cottingham's, for the whole of the *ton* had turned out to congratulate Charles and Amanda. The costumes were mostly rich and elaborate so the ladies could flaunt their jewels, which only accented the elegant simplicity of Amanda's gown.

Mindful of the pike he carried to complete his costume, Andrew wove his way through the crowd looking for Teddy, appropriately dressed as a jester. He found him at last and roared with laughter, for he sat glumly, his legs folded beneath him and his chin in his hands, at his mother's feet. The Duchess of Braxton was dressed as a medieval queen, and held in her hand a leash attached to the loose collar buckled around the neck of her court fool.

"This ain't funny," Teddy said, the bells on his hat jingling as he glanced up at him sourly.

"But it is your just desserts," Andrew replied unsympathetically, and took up a yeoman-like stance next to the duchess as his parents approached.

"And there will be no throwing spokes in anyone's wheel this evening," Her Grace said sternly, and gave the leash a shake, "for I shall know where you are at every moment."

"Eugenia," Lord Hampton said to her anxiously in a low voice. "Was Charles successful?"

"I'm not at all certain," she replied worriedly.

"He received a message shortly after the guests began to arrive, but I've no idea what it said." She
sighed, surveying the packed ballroom. "I suppose
we should begin the dancing or people will begin to
wonder."

Her Grace nodded to the orchestra leader, who'd
been awaiting her signal, and the music began. It
was a waltz, and the floor cleared, but for Charles
and Amanda. Though Caesar stumbled once or
twice—whether over the steps or his toga, Andrew
couldn't tell—there wasn't so much as a twitter
from the crowd. His empress smiled up at him
fondly, indulgently, yet somewhat wanly.

Andrew heard it, and felt a rush of gooseflesh up
his back as the opening bars repeated, and other
couples swung onto the floor in time to the music.
He glanced around quickly, but because no one else
seemed to be reacting, he thought he'd imagined
it—until Lucifer burst through the open French
doors that gave onto the terrace.

His piercing whinney and the clatter of his hooves
on the marble floor drew a bleat of jarring, screech-
ing notes from the startled musicians, and a round
of shrieks from the crowd. When he rose halfway
on his hindlegs, laid back his ears, and bugled deep
in his chest, the dancers scattered. All but Charles
and Amanda, who turned to face the stallion and
the man in the black silk mask on his back.

His sister's lips moved, and though Andrew was
too far away to hear the words, he knew she murmured "my dearest darling." Behind her, his laurel
wreath askew, Charles stood grinning from ear to
ear, until Lucifer danced sideways, and Lesley drew
his rapier. The ring of the blade drawing free of its
scabbard brought a gasp from the guests, and a
stricken look to the duke's face.

For a moment, Lesley held the rapier at his side, then tossed it into the air. It turned end over end as it fell, the light from the chandeliers sliding up the blade and winking on the hilt. When it landed with a clatter a safe distance away, Charles sighed audibly and went limp with relief.

"Bennett, shouldn't you do something?" Lady Hampton twittered nervously. "I thought it was Lesley we were expecting."

"It *is*, Cornelia," Lord Hampton growled, and Andrew heard the clap of his father's hand over his mother's mouth.

Then Lesley tugged off his mask and flung it toward Amanda, his name rippling through the crowd on a murmur of disbelief. A tremulous smile quavering on her lips, she picked it up and ran it lightly through her fingers, her glimmering eyes fixed on Lesley's face. For a moment there was only the jingle of Lucifer's bit and the clash of his hooves on the floor, then Amanda was running toward him, the guests were gasping in horror, and Teddy was leaping and whooping at the end of his leash.

Grinning and leaning down from his saddle, Lesley caught her in one arm and swooped her up in front of him. With a shrill whinney, Lucifer spun toward the doors on his hindlegs, giving Andrew a glimpse of the shining smile on his sister's face before he leaped away into the darkness.

Pandemonium broke out in his wake, but mostly among the Earnshaw and Gilbertson families. Dumbfounded as the guests were by the shocking abduction they'd just seen, they were even more taken aback when the Duchess of Braxton hiked up her skirts and shouted to the orchestra, "Play something lively!"

She cast off Teddy's leash, and Andrew threw

down his pike. Lord Hampton whirled the duchess in a giddy circle, Charles tossed his laurel wreath into the air, grabbed a stunned Lady Hampton and pranced her around the floor.

While Andrew and Teddy, linking elbows and laughing, jigged about like two drunken sailors, Lesley reined Lucifer beneath the beech tree in the farthermost corner of the garden, where a lantern lit and hung from one of the lower branches made a soft pool of tallowy light.

"No more masks," he said firmly, untying the ribands securing the one Charles had sent with Amanda's costume.

He loosened the tight coils Marie had put in her hair as he did so, then tossed the mask away, and tenderly cupped her face in his hands.

"I love you, Amanda Gilbertson."

"I love you, Lesley Earnshaw."

"Even though I deceived you? Twice?"

"Yes," she replied, a mischevious glint coming into her eyes. "But there'd better not be a third time."

"Never again, my darling," he promised, and kissed her.

It was the kiss he'd never thought to give her, the kiss that had tormented him until Charles's messenger had found him earlier that day at their father's hunting box. Being there had been torture; torture he'd thought he deserved, and that now made the quiver of Amanda's mouth against his even sweeter.

"My dearest darling," she sighed contentedly, once he'd released her and folded her into his arms.

"I was terrified you wouldn't come to me when you saw it was my face behind the mask," Lesley murmured into her hair.

"I might not have," Amanda admitted, tipping back her head to smile at him, "if Charles hadn't told me it was you, and Mr. Fisk hadn't explained your pact with him."

"But how did Charles—"

"He recognized Lucifer."

Beneath them, the stallion snorted and stamped his hooves.

"You are aware, are you not," Lesley asked with a grin, "that this is the second time I've compromised you?"

"And *you* are aware, are you not," Amanda returned happily, "that you absolutely *must* marry me this time?"

"Oh, definitely," he returned agreeably. "It's why I made sure the whole of the *ton* was present to witness your ruination."

"You are a wicked man, Lesley Earnshaw," Amanda laughed.

"I *was* a wicked man," he corrected her. "For tonight is the last time Captain Rakehell will ride."

"Before you go, captain, I have one last question." Amanda smiled up at him playfully. "Just exactly where were you wounded?"

"Why, Waterloo, of course."

"Not *that* where." Amanda made a face at him. "The *other* where."

"Never you mind, for now." Lesley kissed the tip of her nose and chuckled. "You'll find out on our wedding night."